THE AL MAK...

Kings o...
Masters of the bedroom!

Razi al Maktabi

This prince has two passions: business and women. His playboy days might be numbered when duty beckons, but there's always time for one final fling! As he takes the Phoenix throne, Razi will work the same magic on the Isla de Sinnebar as he has on every woman of marriageable age—but what happens when he finds out he's going to be a father?

Razi was last seen cavorting in RULING SHEIKH, UNRULY MISTRESS in Mills & Boon® Modern Heat™!

Ra'id al Maktabi

Darker than night and twice as dangerous, Razi's older brother sits on the Sapphire throne of Sinnebar. Scarred inside and out, Ra'id is a powerhouse of strength and command. He rules his heart like his country—with an iron will. Now one woman is about to come between him and his throne!

Find Ra'id ruling in Mills & Boon® Modern™ Romance!

Ra'id strode across the beach, holding Antonia in his arms as if she weighed nothing, while she linked her hands behind his neck and snuggled her face against his chest. It was the easiest thing in the world to believe they belonged together, and that this was their island with no outside world to complicate or muddy the water.

There was no tomorrow here, no yesterday— there was only now, with the ocean lapping rhythmically on a sugar sand shore, and a sickle moon and diamond stars to light their way. There was just one man, one woman...

There was only this...

MASTER OF THE DESERT

BY
SUSAN STEPHENS

First published in Great Britain 2010
Harlequin Mills & Boon Limited,
Eton House, 18-24 Paradise Road, Richmond, Surrey TW9 1SR

© Susan Stephens 2010

ISBN: 978 0 263 87789 2

Harlequin Mills & Boon policy is to use papers that are natural, renewable and recyclable products and made from wood grown in sustainable forests. The logging and manufacturing process conform to the legal environmental regulations of the country of origin.

Printed and bound in Spain
by Litografia Rosés, S.A., Barcelona

Susan Stephens was a professional singer before meeting her husband on the tiny Mediterranean island of Malta. In true Modern™ Romance style they met on Monday, became engaged on Friday, and were married three months after that. Almost thirty years and three children later, they are still in love. (Susan does not advise her children to return home one day with a similar story, as she may not take the news with the same fortitude as her own mother!)

Susan had written several non-fiction books when fate took a hand. At a charity costume ball there was an after-dinner auction. One of the lots, 'Spend a Day with an Author', had been donated by Mills & Boon® author Penny Jordan. Susan's husband bought this lot, and Penny was to become not just a great friend but a wonderful mentor, who encouraged Susan to write romance.

Susan loves her family, her pets, her friends and her writing. She enjoys entertaining, travel, and going to the theatre. She reads, cooks, and plays the piano to relax, and can occasionally be found throwing herself off mountains on a pair of skis or galloping through the countryside. Visit Susan's website: www.susanstephens.net—she loves to hear from her readers all around the world!

Susan Stephens also writes for
Mills & Boon® Modern Heat™ !

CHAPTER ONE

SHE had the figure of a glamour model, the face of an angel—and she was threatening him with a knife.

It wasn't every day his ocean-going yacht was boarded by a barely clothed virago. What few clothes remained on the young girl's bruised and scratched body were ripped and sodden, and the knife she was brandishing looked as if it had come from his galley. In her other hand, she was holding a hunk of bread and cheese, stolen from the same place, he presumed.

Was a French baguette worth killing for?

Probably, he mused, remembering he had persuaded a top French *boulanger* to open a branch in Sinnebar.

As the merciless sun sliced its way through the mist, his first impulse was to get the pirate princess into the shade, but he remained still, not wanting to provoke her into anything more reckless than she had already attempted. She was young, barely out of her teens, but had clearly been through some sort of trauma. He took in the tangled mass of blonde hair and bruised face with slanting blue-green eyes, more wounded than wounding. 'What do you think you're doing?' he said calmly.

'Don't!' she threatened, jabbing the sultry air with her knife.

He held the laugh, relieved she was okay. Mist hung tenaciously, making visibility poor; she must have climbed up on deck while he'd been in the sea checking the hull for storm damage.

'I'm warning you!' she exclaimed, though he hadn't moved.

If she backed away another inch, she'd be over the side.

Her shock at seeing him had forced her into the role of aggressor, he concluded, remaining still so as not to alarm her. She hadn't recognised him or she would have put down her little knife. 'Why don't you give me the knife?' he suggested, knowing if she had meant to attack him she would have done so by now. 'Or, better still, throw it overboard?'

She bared her teeth at that to give him a little warning growl, like a kitten with a toothache. 'Don't you come any closer,' she warned, 'Or I'll—'

'You'll what?' He disarmed her in one absurdly easy move. There was a flash of warm flesh beneath his hands, then it was all shrieking and clawing as she fought him as if to the death. 'Wildcat!' he exclaimed, feeling a sharp thrill of pain as she dug her sharp, white teeth into his hand. Resigned to capture, she couldn't take her eyes off the much bigger knife he wore hanging from his belt. 'I have no intention of harming you,' he reassured her.

She had no intention of listening, which left him dealing with a wriggling desperado, who drummed his deck furiously with her tiny heels as he steered her towards the opening leading to the lower deck and his first-aid kit.

Finally losing patience, he bound her arms to her side and swung her over his shoulder. 'Stop that!' he instructed as she arched her body and pummelled his back. 'Do you want to bang your head?'

She went rigid as he padded sure-footed below deck into what was an all-purpose space on the ocean-going racing yacht. She was still in shock, he registered as he set her down on the one and only seat. All home comforts had been stripped away below deck to make room for necessary equipment, but as he'd been trialling on this voyage rather than racing there was plenty of fresh food on board—hence the bread his pirate wench had stolen. He had brought other supplies and small comforts along to make his time aboard more pleasurable, including the cushions he'd laid out on deck so he could sleep beneath the stars.

When the girl groaned and put her head in her hands, his first thought was to rehydrate her. He reached into the cold box for a glucose drink. 'Here,' he said, loosening the top and offering it to her. Her expression didn't change. She remained stiffly non-responsive, staring ahead with her jaw set in white-faced fright.

'Drink it, or I'll hold your nose and pour it down your throat.' He'd used similar shock tactics years back when his younger brother Razi had refused to take his medicine.

Just like then, she retaliated with a furious, 'You wouldn't dare!'

One look from him was enough to settle that argument. She held out her hand. He gave her the bottle; she gulped down the contents greedily.

'When was the last time you had something to drink?'

She refused to answer. Swiping the back of her hand across her mouth, she raised blue-green eyes to his face. Chips of glacial ice would have held more heat.

No surrender, he concluded. And as for apologising for trespassing on his yacht? Forget it.

Tugging on the first top that came to hand, he began heating water to bathe her wounds. Blocking her escape with his body, he reached into a cupboard for antiseptic, lint and cotton wool. Adding a splash of disinfectant to the water, he stuffed a blanket under his arm and turned around. 'Here—put this round you.'

She flinched and refused to look at him, drawing her legs in defensively, but it was when she crossed her arms over her chest that he finally lost patience. 'I'm not interested in your body,' he assured her, only to be rewarded by a tiny squeak of protest from a girl who was clearly accustomed to being admired. Proving the point, he put the bowl down and tugged the blanket tightly round her slender shoulders, trying not to notice that one lush, pert breast was partially exposed.

Seeing his momentary distraction, she snatched the blanket from him, holding it so tightly closed that her knuckles turned white.

'Don't flatter yourself.'

She was safe from him—too young, too reckless, plus he resented the intrusion. Any other time or place and he would have had her removed from his presence.

But she was tougher than she looked or she would have been reduced to a hysterical mess by now. She was an irritation, but she was also courageous, he concluded, and a breath of fresh air after the painted harpies who regularly served themselves up at court for his perusal.

There was only one thing wrong with the girl: she reminded him of someone else. Those tangled locks and slanting eyes held an echo of his father's mistress, a woman who had destroyed his mother's life and who had referred to Razi—the step-brother he couldn't have loved more if they had shared the same blood—as the worst mistake she had ever made. That woman might be dead now, but she had left disaster in her wake, and as far as he was concerned she had defined his father's weakness. It had been a fatal weakness that had stolen his father's attention away from his country and its people. With that lesson guiding him, things had changed for the better since he had assumed control. There was no longer chaos in Sinnebar, and his people knew that he would never repeat his father's mistake and become a slave to his heart.

He refocused as the girl shifted restlessly on the bench. 'I'm going to bathe your scratches before they turn septic,' he informed her crisply.

She recognised a command, but to his astonishment something in her eyes said she would dearly like to strike him. 'I wouldn't do that if I were you,' he warned grimly, at which she scowled and slumped back like the spoiled teen he thought her to be. 'When did you last eat?' he demanded as he assessed her wounds and general condition.

Her stomach answered this question with an imperative growl, and then he remembered the hunk of bread she'd dropped on the deck. 'When I've finished, you can eat.'

She tilted her chin at a defiant angle to stare haughtily past him.

So, let her go hungry—though he was forced to concede he admired her nerve. He liked the electricity between them too, but neither of these things would affect how he dealt with her. He would administer basic first-aid and then turn her over to the authorities. 'Arms,' he prompted brusquely, and then, deciding he would teach her what it meant to risk her life in the Gulf, he demanded, 'Don't you know anything about maritime law?'

Her flickering gaze suggested not.

'If I report your actions to the ruling Sheikh in Sinnebar… You have heard of the man known as the "Sword of Vengeance", I take it?' He had the satisfaction of seeing her pale. 'If I tell him that you came aboard my yacht, stole my food and threatened me with one of my own knives I would imagine the most lenient sentence he could hand out would be life imprisonment.'

'But you wouldn't!'

Even as she protested her eyes were narrowing in defiance. He liked her fire. He liked her voice. He liked… 'Report you?' he rapped, calling his wayward thoughts back to order. 'That depends on you telling me exactly how you got here. And be completely honest with me; I shall know at once if you lie.'

Hearing the menace in his voice, she slowly unfurled her legs as if deciding a temporary truce was her only option. 'You were moored up, and so I thought…'

She'd take her chances, he silently supplied, feeling a beat of lust as she held his gaze. She spoke English well, but with the faintest of Italian accents. 'You don't look Italian,' he said, dropping it in casually.

'I had an English mother,' she explained, before her mouth clamped shut, as if she felt she'd said too much.

'Start by telling me what brought you to the Gulf and how you arrived on my yacht.'

'I jumped overboard and swam.'

'You swam?' He weighed up her guarded expression. 'You're telling me you jumped overboard and swam through these seas?' His tone of voice reflected his disbelief.

'For what felt like hours.' She blurted this, and then fell silent.

'Go on,' he prompted, continuing to bathe her wounds.

'Before the mist closed in, the boat we were on was hugging the coastline.'

'"We"?'

She shook her head as if it was important to concentrate. 'I could see this island and was confident I could make it to the shore.'

'You must swim well,' he commented.

'I do.'

She spoke without pride, and, taking in her lithe strength, he was tempted to believe her. But she must have swum like an athlete to survive the storm, and however capable she believed herself to be she was no match for the dangerous currents and unpredictable weather conditions in the waters of the Gulf.

The girl had stirred some instinct in him, he realised. It was the instinct to protect and defend, and he hadn't felt that so strongly since his brother Razi had been young. 'What made you jump overboard?' He had his own suspicions, but wanted to hear it from the girl.

Her face grew strained as she remembered. 'Our boat was attacked.'

'I'll need more than that.' If his suspicions were correct, his security forces would need all the information he could glean from her. 'Was your boat attacked by pirates?'

'How do you know that?' The terror in her eyes suggested she thought he was one of them. In fairness, she had had quite an experience, and he was tempted to comfort her. It was an impulse he resisted.

'I suspected as much, and you just confirmed it. And I'm not a criminal,' he added when she continued to stare at him as if he had just grown horns. 'Quite the contrary—I bring people to justice.'

'So you're a law-enforcement officer?'

'Something like that,' he agreed.

Partially reassured, she settled back. 'I was lucky to escape with my life,' she said, echoing his thoughts exactly. 'I escaped.'

And now she was over-doing it with a dramatic hitch in her voice. As she looked at him, as if trying to gauge his reaction, he suspected she was used to playing someone—an older brother, perhaps? She was out of luck with him. He wasn't so easily won over. 'You are lucky to have escaped with your life—and I'm not talking about the pirates now. You boarded my yacht without permission. I carry arms on board and wouldn't hesitate to use them. What use would your little knife have been to you then?'

Colour rushed to her cheeks while her intelligent eyes sparkled like aquamarines. He didn't need a further reminder to put some distance between them. He picked up the radio, to call the officer on duty and let him know the girl had been found and was safe—and when he turned to look at her he felt another bolt of lust.

She couldn't stop shaking and the man didn't help. She had never imagined such a combination of brutal strength and keen intelligence existed, let alone in such a perfectly sculpted form. His manner was proud—disdainful, even. He was magnificent. He only had to touch her for her body to react as if he was caressing her intimately. There was just one thing wrong. She could be as bold and determined as she liked, but she was way out of her depth here, and he frightened her. She was a flirt, a tease, and was used to getting her own way, but she had never met a man so hard—so hard on *her*. She wasn't used to indifference. She was spoiled—she was the first to admit it—spoiled, both by a brother who adored her and by the attention of half the world's men. If anything, there were times when she wished herself invisible. This was not one of those times.

But why should the man be interested in her? He was out of her league—older, tougher, better looking and more experienced in every way. She had left her comfortable cocoon back in Rome to learn about life, but never had she anticipated learning quite so much quite so fast. She didn't even know if this man was more trustworthy than the pirates, and only had the fact that he had bathed her wounds to go on. Would he have done that if he had intended to harm her?

However caring that might make him seem, she refused to be reassured, or to relax her guard. There was something dangerous about him. At least when the pirates had attacked she'd had the chance to jump overboard, but she suspected this man had lightning reflexes and slept with one eye open. Right now he was talking on the radio in a husky tongue she guessed must be Sinnebalese. She had studied the language before setting out on her journey, and could pick up a word or two, but frustratingly not enough. She could learn more from his manner, Antonia decided, which was brisk, to the point and carried an air of authority. He was someone important—someone people listened to—but who?

He made no allowances for the fact that she was young and vulnerable, and she couldn't decide if she liked that or not. Her brother smothered her, believing she required his constant supervision, whereas this man was more like a warrior from one of her fantasies, and had no time to waste on indulging her. Tall, dark and formidably built, in her dreams she would think of him as a dark master of the night, intense and ruthless, the ultimate prize—in reality, he made her wish she had never left home.

She continued to watch him furtively through a curtain of hair. She'd had no alternative but to board his yacht. She had swum to the point of exhaustion, and when she'd seen his boat looming out of the mist she hadn't thought twice about seizing her chance.

As soon as he finished the call, she quickly drew up her feet and locked her arms around her knees, burying her head to avoid his penetrating stare. But he was ignoring her again, she realised, peeping at him.

She studied him some more as he moved about the cabin. He was spectacularly good-looking, with deeply bronzed skin and wild, black hair that caught on his stubble. The firm, expressive mouth, the earring, the look in his eyes, his menacing form all contributed to the air of danger surrounding him. He might look like her ideal man, but this was not one of her fantasies, and she was so far out of her comfort zone she was having to make up the rules as she went along. But there was no question he could melt hearts from Hollywood to Hindustan, and would certainly make a great Hollywood pirate, with those sweeping, ebony brows and that aquiline nose.

Then she remembered that real pirates were scrawny, smelly, ugly and mean.

As she whimpered at the memory of them, he whirled around. 'What's wrong with you now?'

'Nothing,' she protested. She'd get no sympathy here.

CHAPTER TWO

'YOU must never put yourself in such a vulnerable position again,' he told the girl sternly.

She looked at him in mute surprise, but he cut her no slack. If he eased up she'd think taking chances in the wilderness was acceptable, whereas he knew that if the visibility had been better, and helicopter gun-ships from his air force had been flying over the yacht when she boarded, his snipers might have shot her.

'My boat was attacked by pirates,' she protested. 'I jumped overboard and swam for my life. What else was I supposed to do?'

He couldn't remember the last time anyone had challenged him. In a world of bowed heads and whispering obedience, it was almost a refreshing change. But the girl's safety came first, and for the pirates to be captured he had to warn her off ever doing anything similar again, and find out everything she could tell him. 'Save the attitude,' he barked, 'And stick to the facts.'

She blinked and rallied determinedly, and as her story unfolded his admiration for her grew. It also made him doubly determined that she must learn from the experience.

'You seem to have confused some romantic notion with reality,' he observed acidly when she paused for breath. 'This part of the Gulf is no holiday resort, and you're lucky these are only scratches.'

It had been a relief to find that none of her injuries was serious and was what he might have expected after hearing she'd jumped overboard. 'This will sting,' he warned, loosening the top on a bottle of iodine. To her credit, she barely flinched as he painted it on. The only sign that it hurt her was a sharp intake of breath. She had beautiful legs, coltish and long, and her skin was lightly tanned, as if she had only recently landed in the Gulf. 'What brought you to these shores—a gap year?'

'Sort of.'

She winced—from fear of discovery that she was doing something she shouldn't, he guessed—but before he could question her she hit him with, 'What brought *you* here?'

No one questioned him. He had to forcefully remind himself that here on this desert island they were anonymous strangers and she couldn't know who he was. He shrugged. 'The storm.'

That was the simple answer. Sailing grounded him; it reminded him he was not only a king but a man, and that the man owed it to his country and his people to go hunting for his humanity from time to time. Whether he would ever be successful in that quest, only history would judge. 'And where did you say you were heading?' he prompted.

'I didn't say, but I'm heading for Sinnebar,' she admitted grudgingly when he held her stare.

She was hiding something, he concluded when her gaze flickered away.

'Do we have to talk now?' she muttered, playing the hard-done-by card.

'If you want the pirates to escape…'

'No, of course I don't,' she declared, staring him full in the face.

'Good. So tell me where the attack took place. Did you get a fix—coordinates?' he pressed when she didn't answer right away.

'I know what you mean,' she flared, but for the first time he thought she seemed disappointed in herself because she couldn't give him the detail he required.

He gathered from what she went on to tell him that the pirates had taken advantage of the poor visibility to target an unsophisticated boat that lacked the latest radar equipment and alarm systems. 'So you weren't sailing your own boat when the pirates attacked?' he guessed.

'No.'

Burying her head in her knees, she tensed, but with the criminals still on the loose this was no time to go easy on her. 'Sit up,' he barked.

She snapped upright, and the look in her eyes suggested she was only now realising she might have jumped from the frying pan into the fire. He felt some sympathy for her. Dressed in cut-off shorts and faded top with a shark knife hanging from his belt, he was hardly a reassuring sight. 'Come on,' he pressed impatiently. 'I need this information now, not sometime next week.'

She bit her lip and then admitted in a voice that was barely audible, 'I hitched a lift on a fishing boat.'

'You hitched?' Words failed him. The girl's naivety

appalled him; the danger she had put herself in defied reason. 'What were you trying to prove?'

'Nothing.'

He doubted that. There would be someone back home she wanted to impress. 'Couldn't you have caught the ferry? Or was that too easy for you?'

'I thought the fishing boat would give me a more authentic experience.'

'More authentic?' he demanded cuttingly. 'So, you're another tourist who thinks you can visit a foreign country with nothing more than your thirst for adventure and a bleeding heart in your survival kit?'

Her face paled. 'It wasn't like that at all.'

'It was exactly like that. And then you wonder why you find yourself in danger? Keep your arms outstretched,' he reminded her when she flinched.

His pulse was thundering with outrage at the thought of pirates in the sea off the shores of Sinnebar, though the girl had his attention too. He looked at her tiny hand and thought her courage all the more remarkable, given her petite frame. She was barely half his size, her skin-tone pale against his bronze. Her quick thinking had saved her, he concluded, and because her boldness was at odds with her fragile appearance the pirates had underestimated her. He would not make the same mistake.

Now she was speaking more, she went on to talk with passion of punishment for the pirates and compensation for the fishermen, which launched another unwelcome surge of arousal which he quickly stamped on. However soft and yielding she felt beneath his hands, her mind was not half so compliant, and he had no room in his life for complications. 'What type of boat did they have? Never mind,' he rapped, impatient to gather as much information as he could before placing a second call to the commander of his naval forces. 'Just tell me the colour.'

'It was a skiff,' she said with mild affront. 'Powerful engine; peeling white paint above the water-line; black below. And the interior was painted a vivid shade of aquamarine.'

'A vivid shade of aquamarine?' he murmured dryly. 'Are you sure?'

'Perfectly sure,' she said, holding his gaze with curiosity, as if surprised to see the humour there. 'Have I told you enough?' she asked as he turned to use the radio.

'More than I expected,' he conceded as he prepared to place the call. 'You did well.'

He could feel the heat of her gaze on his back as he fired off orders. He had become part of her desert fantasy, he guessed. Too bad; he wasn't interested. There were plenty of women who knew the score, and this girl wasn't one of them. Breaking radio connection, he turned to face her again.

'Okay?' she said hopefully.

'Okay,' he confirmed. 'So now it's all about you.' He ran a cool stare over her. 'Let's start with your name and what you're doing here.'

No name. She could have no name. Signorina Antonia Ruggiero *must* have no name. Whoever he was, this man was successful; successful people knew other people. And people talked. How good would it look for her to be branded a thief? Or, worse still, a demented creature with a knife? Before she'd even begun the work she'd set out to do.

'You're European,' the man observed in a voice that

strummed something deep inside her. 'Although, like me, I suspect you were educated in England. Am I right?'

She took in the fact that his husky, confident baritone was barely accented even though he had spoken Sinnebalese fluently. 'Yes, that's right.' Her own voice sounded hoarse.

'Where in England were you educated?' His keen eyes watched her closely, and the intensity of expression in those eyes warned her not to lie to him.

'I went to school in Ascot.'

'Ascot?' There was a faint note of mockery in his voice. He'd heard of the very expensive girls' school there. 'So you're a very proper young lady?'

Not in her head. One flash of this man's muscular back when he changed his top confirmed she was anything but proper. 'I try,' she said primly.

'What is such a well-brought-up young lady doing on my yacht, stealing my food and threatening me with a knife?'

His relentless stare sent ribbons of sensation flooding through her, making it hard to concentrate—but this was her best, maybe her only, chance to get to the mainland and it was crucial to forge a relationship with him. She also had to persuade him not to report her to the authorities to avoid being arrested the moment she landed. 'I was hungry— thirsty. Your yacht was here; I took my chances.'

She flinched when he laughed. Short and sharp, it held no hint of humour.

'You certainly did,' he agreed. 'Didn't you think to call out when you came on board? You could have made some attempt to locate the owner before you stole his food.'

'I did call out, but no one answered.'

His lips curved as he propped his hip against the bench

where she was sitting. 'So you helped yourself to whatever you felt like?'

'I didn't touch anything outside the galley.' Must he move so close and tower over her?

'And that makes it right?'

'I'm sorry.' She sounded childlike—plaintive, even—but was lost for something else to say.

'Next time I'm in Ascot, I'll wander into your house and see what I fancy taking, shall I?'

'I don't live in Ascot.' The angry words shot from her mouth without any assistance from her brain and her reward was an ironic grin.

'So, we've ruled out Ascot,' he said.

Before he could delve any further, she swayed and clutched her throat.

'Feeling faint?' he demanded caustically, refusing to be fooled by her amateur dramatics for a single moment.

'I'm fine,' she assured him, matching him stare for stare. Whatever it took, she wasn't about to let him see how badly he affected her.

'You're not fine,' he argued, narrowing his eyes. 'You've had a shock and need time to get over it.'

She hoped that meant a reprieve, and shrank instinctively from his intense maleness as he eased away from the bench.

'Relax.' His lips tugged with very masculine amusement. 'You're safe with me.'

Did he mean that to be reassuring, or was he insulting her? And *was* she safe? Could he be trusted? For once, she didn't know what to think. The man's manner was dismissive and abrupt, and his appearance… Well, that was rather more intimidating than the pirates.

There could be no guarantees, Antonia concluded, even if he had bathed her wounds. So was the flutter inside her chest a warning to be on her guard, or awareness of his sexuality?

'Are you travelling alone?'

A shiver of apprehension coursed through her as she stared into his eyes. Why would he ask that? 'Yes,' she admitted cautiously. 'I'm travelling alone—but people know where I am.'

'Of course they do,' he said sarcastically. 'So your family allows you to wander the world without their protection?'

This time she couldn't hold back. 'They trust me.' She was not defending herself now, but Rigo, the older brother who had cared for her since her mother had died six months after giving birth to her, her father having passed away shortly after that.

But the man pursued her relentlessly. 'And breaking the law is how you repay your family for their care?'

'I've already apologised to you for coming on board,' she fired back. 'I explained I had no option but to board your yacht.'

His hands signalled calm as her voice rose. 'Lucky for you I was moored up here.'

She balled her hands into fists as a last-ditch attempt to keep her temper under control, but all it gained her was another mocking stare. But *what* a stare… She couldn't help wondering how it would feel to have that stare fire with interest, or darken with desire.

'I hope you've learned your lesson,' he snapped, shattering that particular illusion.

'Oh, I have,' she assured him meekly. It was time to stop dreaming and accept the facts. She was far too young and inexperienced to interest a man like this. He thought her fragile and foolish, and couldn't know her determination. She wasn't fragile, and this trip was her chance to prove she wasn't foolish. To prove to the brother she adored—who protected her, perhaps a little too much—that she could survive without his supervision. Not that she'd made the best of starts, Antonia conceded as the man held her gaze.

'Tell me more about your family,' he prompted.

Being the object of such an intense stare was both alarming and seductive, but she wouldn't tell him anything that might risk her mission. She hadn't come to Sinnebar on her own behalf, or as part of some ill-thought-out adventure, but to persuade the authorities in the country to open a branch of her brother's children's charity. Rigo's work had already helped so many sick and disadvantaged children, and she had pledged to help him expand the reach of his charity across the world.

And there was a second reason, Antonia conceded silently. Coming to Sinnebar would give her the opportunity to track down information about the mother it broke her heart to think she couldn't remember—not her voice, her touch, what she looked like or even the scent of her hair. She knew nothing at all about the woman who had given birth to her, beyond the fact that her mother had been very young when she'd died, and that before marrying Antonia's father and moving to Rome she had apparently spent some time at the royal court in Sinnebar.

'I'm waiting to hear about your family,' the man said, slicing through her thoughts.

Antonia composed herself before replying, knowing it was important not to let anything slip. Rigo had drummed it into her from an early age that the truth was non-negotiable, though she might have to get used to twisting it where this man was concerned. 'My family don't know I'm here,' she admitted, which was true in part, at least.

'Your family don't know you're here?' The man picked up the radio phone and held it out to her. 'Don't you think you'd better call them?'

No. Men like this, men like her brother Rigo, shared a common understanding. They would demand she return home immediately. Rigo might even insist on coming to fetch her, so once again she would be no more effective than a balloon, weightless and directionless as they batted her between them.

'I'll ring them if you don't,' he threatened.

'No, please don't.' She reached out and then withdrew her hand, thinking better of touching him. 'I don't want to worry them.' She mustered a steady stare. 'Better to call them when I'm safely in Sinnebar and settled in a hotel, don't you think?'

Worry them? Rigo would be down on her like a ton of bricks. Her brother only had to file a flight plan and he'd be over here. And what would that prove—that she was as headstrong and reckless as Rigo believed her to be? Her brother would never let her work for his charity then. And she had begged him for this chance to do a real job instead of accepting her brother's generous allowance. It was a chance to do something for others instead of for herself. 'The moment I'm safe on the mainland, I'll ring them—I promise.' She was taking a lot for granted by assuming the man would take her anywhere, but she had no option when there was everything to play for.

His eyes remained narrowed with suspicion, and then
to her relief he shrugged. 'You know your family better
than I do.'

Yes, she knew Rigo. He could be a pain sometimes, but
it was thanks to her brother she had enjoyed such a privi-
leged childhood, which in Rigo's language meant she could
ride, ski, sail, fence and swim. More importantly, living
with him had taught her how to survive a man like this.

As she watched him clear up the debris from the recent
triage session, she offered to help. He ignored her. Closing
the cupboard on his supplies, he turned to face her. 'So all
you wanted when you came on board was my food?'

'What else?' she said in bewilderment.

'You weren't thinking of stealing my yacht, for instance?'

Antonia's cheeks flushed red. She *had* considered it.

He made a contemptuous sound, as if he already knew
this, and then barked, 'We'll continue this conversation
when you have no more excuses left.'

'But, I—'

'Not now,' he snarled.

His tone only confirmed what she already knew—this
was not a man to bend to her will, or to anyone's will.

'You will rest now,' he said as if anything he commanded would happen immediately. 'I'm prepared to give
you time to get over the shock—but not much time. And
don't play me,' he warned.

A shiver of awareness rippled down her spine. When he
turned away, it was another opportunity to watch him
again. Resting her chin on her knees, she realised that
against all the odds she had grown calmer around him.
Calmer and yet more unsettled, Antonia concluded, real-

ising her libido had received an unusual boost. The man moved around the confined space with the confidence of someone who knew every inch of his territory intimately, and some of the openings were so small he had to raise his arms and coax his body through. He looked amazing at full stretch, like an athlete in the peak of condition. His air of command went with being super-fit, she supposed, though she found trying to pigeon-hole him in the outside world impossible. His frayed and faded shorts looked as if he'd hacked the legs off an old pair of jeans with the lethal-looking knife hanging from his belt, and his top had definitely seen better days.

She gave up trying to work him out. He could be crew or he could own the boat—either way, she had to build bridges and hope they stretched to the mainland. She waited until the next time he squeezed past to attempt to make her peace. 'I apologise for trespassing on your yacht and for stealing your food and the knife. Please believe me when I say I would never have used the knife. And please don't report me to the Sheikh.'

'I thought I told you to rest,' he said, showing no sign of having accepted her apology.

There was no chance of 'playing him', as he seemed to think, Antonia concluded, and he'd done nothing more than care for her as he would care for a stray dog, so she could forget the fantasies. Using her so-called womanly wiles had got her nowhere. And there was something more, something that made her shudder to think about it. While he was helping her, she was safe, but should he ever turn against her...

'What happens next is up to you,' he snapped as if he

had read these troubled thoughts. 'All you have to do is answer my questions promptly and honestly.'

And that was all? Did he know how intimidating and fierce he looked? 'I will,' she promised on a dry throat. *If all your questions are connected to the attack*, she hedged silently.

CHAPTER THREE

THE man might terrify her, but she was determined to hold her nerve; so much depended on getting to the mainland. If only she knew who he was it might be easier to talk to him, but she had searched for clues to his identity and found none on the yacht. There was plenty of food and drink in the tiny galley and all sorts of fancy technical equipment—and, now she put her shopping head on, she realised the blanket around her shoulder was cashmere. But the man remained a mystery. Apart from his working clothes, he wore a strap around his wrist formed of black twine, and the gold hoop in his ear which she found sexy, but neither item was unique.

It wasn't much to go on. She should have noticed the name of his yacht, but she had been so traumatised when she'd clambered on board her thoughts had been solely concerned with survival. She hadn't even paused to think who the yacht might belong to. Food, drink and a fast ticket back to the mainland had been her only concern. And if she had to steal a sleek, sexy racing yacht to get there, so be it.

'I don't have all day,' he warned. 'The least you can do is tell me why you're here.'

Even if she had been prepared to tell him the truth it was hard to think straight with his sexuality overwhelming her. Command was instinctive for him, while she was a girl used to getting her own way; theirs could be an explosive partnership.

In the realms of fantasy only, Antonia cautioned herself firmly. She had been so absorbed in sleuthing it took her a moment to realise that he was holding out the most delicious-looking baguette. Slathered in butter, it had a wedge of cheese inside it so thick it would normally have fed her for a week. And she hadn't eaten for… She couldn't remember.

'Is that for me?' She granted him the first smile of the day as she reached for it.

He held it out of reach. 'Talk first,' he said brusquely. 'You've had enough time to collect your thoughts. And if you can't remember your own name…' A quirk of his eyebrow was all it took to call her a liar. 'Why don't you start with your parents' names?'

'Both my parents are dead.'

'And they had no name either, I suppose?'

Had she expected sympathy? Antonia's skin prickled at this evidence of a man who was cold and remote. It under-scored what she had already sensed about him, that you wouldn't want him as an enemy, and as she stared into his eyes she wondered if she had never met anyone so removed from human feeling. He unnerved her to the point that she felt like voicing her mother's name, almost as if it were a talisman that could protect her. But her mother's name was too precious for that, and so she attempted a little sob instead. 'Please, let me eat first. I'm s-so hungry…'

There was a moment of silence between them, and

then, as if she had planned it, her stomach growled in anguish. 'Please…'

She must have paled or swayed, or gasped for breath; all three were possible when the man was so close to her. 'Eat, then talk,' he conceded brusquely, handing over the baguette.

She dropped her gaze to hide her relief as she crammed the delicious roll into her mouth, going to heaven and back in the space of a couple of gargantuan bites.

'Steady—drink something.'

He took the top off a bottle of water, which she grabbed from him gracelessly and gulped down.

'Take a few minutes to let the food settle.'

His words might have seemed considerate, but the look on his face was not. He was telling her she had better not take longer than he expected to pull herself round. Brusque or not, his manner thrilled her. Why did it always have to be the pretty boys who wanted her, when what she wanted was a real man who could stare her in the eyes—a man like this man, who made her body tremble?

Clearly, his thoughts were not running in tandem with her. Far from returning her interest, he simply dumped another blanket on top of her in passing. He couldn't have been more unromantic if he'd tried, while her head was full of him touching her in quite a different way.

'You need to sleep,' he said brusquely. 'You're still in shock. We'll talk later.'

Sleep? Was he serious? He obviously thought he only had to issue a command and her eyes would close immediately. 'Sleep here?' She stared dubiously at the narrow bunk.

'Yes, of course here,' he rapped with a frown that would have sent grown men scurrying for cover.

'I'm not sure I can sleep,' she said honestly.

'You can try,' he insisted.

She reluctantly dragged the blanket close. Like the man, it held the fresh tang of the ocean, and like him it felt wonderful against her skin. But as she curled up on the bunk all her bravado fell away, leaving just longing and loneliness. However formidable he seemed, and however much of a threat he posed, he had made her feel safe. And that was such a good feeling, Antonia reflected, biting back tears.

She was physically and mentally exhausted, Antonia reasoned, impatient with herself for the weakness. Her emotions were in tatters, and no wonder, when in the short space of time she'd known him this brute of a man had turned her life plan on its head. She'd carried a mental image with her of returning to Rome in triumph after opening branches of Rigo's charity across the Middle East. Eventually, she would return home and settle down— probably with some nice, safe man her brother had chosen for her. After which, life would go on pretty much as it always had, with lots of pats on the head for Antonia and not too many problems to worry her. And of course, her husband, like her brother, would adore her.

But now…

How was she supposed to lose her innocence to some lesser man now? The man had ruined her prospects of a nice, cosy future. And as for sex…

'Relax,' he insisted as she squirmed beneath the blanket. 'No one's going to touch you while I'm around.'

Especially not him, she gathered.

Throwing herself down on the bunk, she stretched out. Why had fate chosen to bring her to the attention of a man

who had turned her world upside down with one contemptuous stare when he wasn't even interested in her?

Tugging the blanket over her head, she determined that
out of sight would mean out of mind—but how was that
supposed to happen when she could hear him moving
about, and when even the sound of his steady pacing was
starting to soothe her? Then incredibly, thanks to the man's
strangely reassuring presence and the gentle rocking of the
boat, her eyes drifted shut and she fell asleep.

His voice was muted, so he didn't wake her as he issued
orders to his Chief of Staff. The girl was sleeping soundly
now, her blonde hair drifting in a curtain of gold to the
floor. He turned away from that distraction to relay every
detail his unexpected guest had been able to recall. When
he ended the call, he went up on deck where a technico-
lour sky would soon darken to the impenetrable mantle of
a desert night.

Time had passed rapidly since the girl's arrival, and as
he paced the deck he realised that just the thought of her
was enough to unsettle him. It was as if the two of them
had created some unusual energy, almost as if together
they possessed the power to forge some new force. Having
been only too glad to turn his back on her, he now found
he was impatient for her to wake up. He wanted to test that
energy to see if she would be like all the rest—outwardly
intriguing, but ultimately shallow.

He remained alert while he paced, and realised now he
was listening for her soft footfall, but all he could hear was
the sigh of a restless sea and the rhythmical chirrup of the
cicadas on shore. Leaning back against the mast, he al-

lowed his thoughts to drift. They returned at once to the mystery girl—her clear, blue-green eyes hazed over with passion and the sight of her begging him for more…

He pulled away from the mast, shaking his head like an angry wolf, as if that could dislodge her from his thoughts. He had already decided she was too young for him.

But she was intriguing.

The trill of the satellite phone provided a welcome distraction, until he learned the purpose of the call. He had ordered that all his late father's palaces be aired and cleaned before being redecorated and opened to the public, and it appeared they had found a locked room today. When his comptroller of palaces went on to advise him that they hadn't been able to locate a key to the room, a thought occurred to him. Was it possible the room had belonged to his father's mistress? There were so many secrets where that woman was concerned.

He commanded that they remove the door from its hinges—or break it down if they had to. Once they had gained access, if it proved to have been her lair, everything she had owned must be taken out and destroyed.

She must have cat-napped; when she woke there was no sign of the man. She guessed he was up on deck and, though sleeping under the stars sounded idyllic to her, she was beginning to feel guilty at the thought that she was taking up his one and only bunk. Sitting up and stretching, she realised it was still relatively early, and that he was unlikely to be asleep.

She wanted to see him again. She wanted to make a fresh start. She wanted him to see her differently. She had been so shocked at their first encounter she had acted foolishly, and hadn't seen anything from his point of view, but now she had slept and felt refreshed she could understand his brusque manner. She was the trespasser, and yet he'd fed her and bathed her wounds. What had she done for him? She must earn her passage back to the mainland as cook, crew, anything he wanted—within reason, of course. The least she could do now was to take him a cooling drink.

The *very* least, Antonia concluded, her heart hammering with anticipation as she padded silently across the deck with a cooling lemonade she had decorated with a slice of lemon, an ice cube and even a sprig of mint she had found in the man's supplies.

The dark shape loomed out of nowhere. She screamed and the drink went flying. The man yanked her in front of him and, dipping his head, demanded, 'Do you never learn?'

She was trembling so much it took her a moment to speak, and then fury and shock turned her intended apology on its head. '"Are you all right?" might be nice,' she raged back at him.

The man was already blazing with affront, which only increased at her outburst. Bringing his face close to hers in the most intimidating way imaginable, he snarled, 'Do yourself a favour and learn how dangerous it is to creep up on me.'

'Well, I'm sorry if I frightened you.'

'Frightened me?' He seemed surprised for a moment, and then, throwing back his head, he laughed, strong white teeth flashing in the moonlight.

She couldn't even bring him a drink without making a mess of things, Antonia seethed inwardly. She could cope in her brother's sophisticated circles in Rome without any trouble at all, but she couldn't seem to get a single thing right where this man was concerned. And now she was in danger of ruining everything and losing her lift to the mainland. 'Look, I'm sorry.'

'Cloth,' he snapped without sparing her a glance.

She bit back an angry retort, accepting he was right on this occasion. She shouldn't have shouted at him or spilled lemonade on his deck. She should have remembered this wasn't some pleasure cruiser and that she was here under sufferance. 'I'll get you a cloth.'

'You bet you will. You made the mess, you clear it up!'

So much for her kind gesture! She should have saved some of the lemonade to toss over him. 'I thought you might want a drink. Was it my fault you leapt out at me? And now you expect me to follow orders like a dog. You'll be whistling for me next.'

'Have you finished?'

His quiet way of speaking drew her attention to his lips. Taking herself out of danger range, she headed below deck at speed. She was going to stick with her original plan, which was to be useful to him so he would be more likely to give her a lift to the mainland.

She returned moments later with a fresh drink, a clean cloth and a new sense of purpose in her step. 'Here,' she said, hanging on to the cloth as she offered him the freshly prepared drink. She was bowed, but not defeated. If she had a hope of reaching Sinnebar, pride was not an option.

'Where are you going?' the man demanded as she carried on walking.

She waved the cloth at him. 'To clean up.'

'Sit down over there,' he ordered, indicating a bulkhead well out of his way. 'And please try not to fall overboard while I make a proper job of clearing up the mess you made.'

So she couldn't even be trusted with a cloth? She hung on to it, expecting every moment he would snatch it from her. 'I'd like to help,' she said bluntly, amazed by the steadiness of her voice. 'I've made a mistake—I know that, I'm pretty clumsy—but I'd like to put it right.'

There was a moment of silence, and then he saluted her with the plastic tumbler. 'Do your worst.'

She saw the glint in his eyes. He was laughing at her, but she kept her temper under control. Apart from the lift she so badly needed, she was playing a very dangerous game with a man she didn't know. There could be no mixing up of dreams and reality here. Placating him was her best, her only, option.

Once she'd cleared up the mess, she faced him again. 'I realise I haven't exactly got off on the best foot.'

She waited for him to contradict her. Any gentleman would. But this man wasn't a gentleman, he was a barbarian, who angled his chin to stare at her with derision as if he were wondering how deep she would care to dig the hole before jumping into it. 'Can we start again?' she suggested, somehow remaining calm.

The sight of one inky eyebrow peaking made her cheeks flame red, but with her lift in serious jeopardy she wasn't about to take any chances. 'I'm prepared to work my passage back to the mainland, if you'll just tell me what you'd like me to do.'

'You could leave me in peace?' he suggested.

Antonia's jaw dropped. She was welcome everywhere.

Except here, she concluded as the man directed a pointed glance at the companionway leading below deck.

'Can I do anything more for you?' he said pointedly.

'Absolutely not,' she assured him, spinning on her heels. She paused at the top of the steps to deliver her exit line: 'You've done quite enough for me already.'

But as she spoke she glimpsed the island behind him. It looked so desolate in the fading light. Did she really want to be stranded there? 'Just for the record, I really am sorry I made such a mess of things and spilled a drink, but you shouldn't have leapt out at me.'

The man's eyes narrowed threateningly.

She tensed and went on, 'I only brought you a drink because—'

'You felt guilty?' He suggested. 'And I'm guessing that's a first for you.'

'You don't know anything about me.'

'I know all I want to know.'

'How can you say that?' Because he didn't want to know any more about her, Antonia realised, heating up with embarrassment. 'What have I ever done to you? Why do you hate me so much?'

'I don't hate you,' he said. 'I don't feel anything that requires that much energy. Let me spell it out for you,' he offered. 'I have neither the time nor the inclination to deal with spoiled brats who march into danger with their eyes wide open, expecting other people to bail them out.'

'It wasn't like that.'

'How would you describe it?'

For once she was lost for words. 'I'm going below.'

'You do that.'

She had never been dismissed by anyone before, and the thought that it was so unjust forced her to turn one last time and confront him. 'Why should I sleep below deck where it's hot and stuffy, while you're up here enjoying the breeze?'

'Have you never been told "thank you, we'll call you" after one of your dramatic performances? No, I guess not,' he said wearily. 'Well, there's a first time for everything, I guess. Off you go,' he prompted with a dismissive gesture.

'I'm staying right here.'

He shrugged, turned his back and walked away.

CHAPTER FOUR

HE WATCHED her out of the corner of his eye. She sat well away from him, glancing at him when she thought he wasn't looking. She reminded him of a newly caged animal taking account of its changed circumstances before making any rash moves. When she realised he was watching her, she quickly looked away.

The light had begun to fade, cloaking them in shadows. The yacht was barely moving, and even the waves had grown lazy as they lapped against the side of the boat, as if the ocean was preparing itself for sleep. Night fell quickly in the desert, and he guessed she would want to freshen up before she had something to eat. Although she had annoyed him intensely, he had no intention of starving her. 'Are you hungry?'

She pretended not to hear him.

She stirred, but refused to look at him. Instead, she stretched out on her back, staring up at the sky, her sun-bleached hair dusting the deck. 'What time is it?' she said as if they were the best of friends.

'Time for you to swim and freshen up, and then we'll eat,' he told her in a tone of voice that gave her no encouragement.

Putting conditions on her chance to eat grabbed her attention. She sat bolt upright, still pretending unconcern as she twisted her hair into an expert knot, which she then secured with a band she wore around her wrist.

Her delicate bone-structure held his interest momentarily. 'Up,' he commanded, shaking the sight of her long, naked limbs out of his head. 'You've been lazing around long enough. What you need now is exercise.'

'To get over the shock?' she challenged him with a glare.

'To stretch your limbs,' he countered, refusing to be sucked in by her 'poor little victim' act. She had been through a trauma, but it wouldn't help her to dwell on it—and he suspected she wasn't as badly affected as she made out, if only because acting was something she could turn on and off at will.

She stood up and stretched. 'A swim?' she said, slanting a blue-green gaze at him. 'I could handle that.'

Shaking his head, he turned away. What was it about this girl that drew him to her? She was a feisty bundle of trouble, and he should know better than to lead her on when he went for mature, gracious women—usually with a title, and always with a keen sense of what was and wasn't correct. Something told him there was nothing remotely correct about this girl.

He should not have suggested she go for a swim. He could count the mistakes he'd made in his adult life on the fingers of one hand and this was up there with the best. Did he need reminding that the girl who had insisted on scrubbing the whole of his deck after mopping up the original spill, and polishing every surface until it gleamed, had the frame of a young gazelle and the bosom of a centrefold, or that plastic surgery had played no part in her good fortune?

He was on shore, preparing a cooking fire, when she walked out of the sea and strolled towards him looking like a nubile film-star in her too-short shorts and ripped top. He steeled himself not to look, but it was already too late when the image was branded on his mind.

Apparently unaware of the effect she was having on him, she came to stand within splashing distance, and, twisting her hair to get rid of the water before flinging it carelessly back, she demanded, 'What are you cooking?'

He gave her a look. 'What does it look like?'

'Fish?'

'Well done.'

'Not too well done, I hope?' she chipped in cheekily, clearly refreshed by her swim. 'You don't like anything about me, do you?' she protested when he slanted an ironic stare in her direction.

She would wait a long time for him to play along with that line. But, actually, she was growing on him. Apart from her obvious attractions, or perhaps in spite of them, beneath her adolescent quirkiness there was real grit and determination. She was uncompromising, he had concluded, like him, and now he sat back to enjoy the show he was sure was about to begin. He didn't have to wait long.

Seeing that she had failed to provoke him, she upped the ante. 'I'm just in the way.' She pulled a broken face. 'You'd far rather be here on your own.'

'Without the cabaret?' He stirred the fire. 'You've got that right.'

While he spoke she was circling him like a young gazelle not quite sure what she was dealing with, until finally curiosity overcame her and she came to peer over his shoulder at the food he was preparing. 'It's got its head on!' she exclaimed as he impaled on a spit the fish he'd just caught.

'They grow that way in the Gulf.'

'Is that the only choice for supper?'

'Did I forget to give you the menu?'

'Stop teasing me,' she protested.

Without any effort on his part a new sense of ease was developing between them. She'd made a bad start, but she had worked really hard since then to make up for it. 'You don't have to eat the fish,' he said, playing along. 'You don't have to eat at all. Or, if you want something off the menu, I'm sure there's plenty more bread in the galley that could do with eating up.'

She scowled at this, but then an uncertain smile lit her face when their glances connected.

They were beginning to get the measure of each other, and both of them liked what they saw, he concluded. He was more relaxed than usual; this was luxury for him, eating simply, cooking the fresh fish he'd caught over an open fire. It gave him a chance to kick back and experience a very different life.

The fish did smell good. And she was ravenous. 'Can we start over?' Antonia suggested, knowing there was more at stake than her first proper meal of the day—her voyage to the mainland, for instance, not to mention sharing a meal with a frighteningly attractive man she dared to believe was starting to warm to her.

'That all depends.'

'I've told you that I'd like to help, and I mean it,' she said. 'I can sail—I can help you sail to the mainland.'

'Help me sail?' he murmured, skimming a gaze over her tiny frame.

'Seriously—let me prove it to you. I'm not as useless as I look.'

He stared into the fire to hide his smile.

'If I knew your name, it would be a start,' she persisted. 'Maybe we could relax around each other more if we knew what to call each other.'

'Wasn't that my question to you?'

Antonia's cheeks blazed. How could she be so careless? Wasn't that the one question she wouldn't answer? 'I have to call you something,' she pressed, getting her question in first.

She had almost given up when he answered, 'You can call me Saif.'

'Saif?' she exclaimed, seizing on the word. 'Doesn't that mean sword in Sinnebalese?' And, without giving him a chance to answer, she rattled on, 'When I first planned to travel to Sinnebar I studied the language.'

Instead of turning things around as she had hoped, this only provoked one of his dismissive gestures. 'The name Saif is very popular in Sinnebar,' he explained, stoking the fire with a very big stick.

'But it isn't your real name?' she said, tearing her gaze away. 'Saif is just a name you've adopted for while you're here,' she guessed.

Please, please say something, she urged him silently. 'If you don't want to tell me your real name, that's all right by me.'

Nothing.

'We could have a name truce,' she pressed as another idea occurred to her.

'What do you mean by that?'

Her confidence grew; imagination was her speciality. 'Our outside lives can't touch us here—you can be Saif, and I can be—'

'I shall call you Tuesday.'

'Tuesday?' She frowned.

'I take it you've heard of Man Friday?'

'Of course I have, but—'

He shrugged. 'You came on board on a Tuesday.'

They were really communicating, and for the first time since she'd come aboard his yacht she could see the light at the end of the tunnel.

Or at least the lighthouse guarding the entrance to the harbour of Sinnebar.

'Tuesday it is, then,' she agreed eagerly. 'Would you like me to fillet the fish for you?' She wanted to prove she could be helpful in so many ways.

Saif paused, knife suspended. His expression reflected his doubt in her abilities. 'All right, go ahead,' he said reluctantly.

And make a mess of it if you dare, Antonia silently translated.

She swallowed as Saif drew his knife, and took it gingerly from him with the thick, beautifully carved pommel facing towards her hand. 'This is very nice,' she said, struggling to wrap her hand around it. 'Is it an heirloom?'

'There's nothing special about it,' Saif said as he removed the fish from the spit he'd made out of twigs and a piece of twine. 'It's a utility item and nothing more.'

'Well, it's a very nice utility item.'

Nothing *special*? Apart from the knife's size, and the fact that it could slice the gizzard out of a shark at a single stroke, it was the most fearsome weapon she had ever seen. And one she would put to good use. Her juices ran as Saif waved the fish on the stick to cool it, sending mouth-watering aromas her way.

It was a relief to discover that all the trips to fabulous restaurants with her brother Rigo hadn't been wasted. Positioning the fish on the large, clean leaf that would act as a plate, she removed the head, skin and bones with a few skilful passes of Saif's razor-sharp blade. 'You first,' she insisted, passing the succulent white morsels of fish to him on their bed of lush emerald-green leaf.

She breathed a sigh of relief when Saif's lips pressed down with approval and he murmured, 'Good work.'

'Thank you.'

'This is delicious,' she observed, tucking in with gusto. 'We make a good team, you and I.'

Careless words, Antonia realised when one arrogant ebony eyebrow peaked. She ate in silence after that, and when they were finished went to rinse her hands in the sea. Sitting down on the sand a safe distance from Saif, she leaned back on her hands to stare at the moon. It wasn't long before she was longing for things she couldn't have— a sexy Arabian lover with a body made for non-stop sin, for instance.

Saif turned when she sighed, but what could she do? It was such a romantic evening. There was a smudge of luminous orange at the horizon, and overhead a candy-striped canvas of pink and aquamarine remained stubbornly in place as the sky darkened into night. 'You don't know how lucky you are living here,' she murmured. 'Though they say the ruling Sheikh is—'

'What?' Saif demanded sharply. 'What do they say about the ruling sheikh?'

From the look on his face, she had over-stepped some unseen boundary. Rolling onto her stomach, she laced her hands beneath her chin, sensing diplomacy was urgently required. 'Surely you know him better than I do?'

'Maybe,' he admitted.

'Aren't you allowed to be rude about him?'

'I can be as rude as I like—but I don't like,' Saif said pointedly, flashing a warning glance her way.

'I'm sorry; I didn't mean to offend you. I just heard he was fierce, that's all.'

Rolling onto her back, she hoped she'd done enough to placate him. She really hadn't meant to offend him. 'Shall we have pudding now?' she suggested, hoping to break the sudden tense silence.

'Pudding?'

She only needed the smallest encouragement. 'Yes— then it will be like a proper picnic.' She sprang up and ran back to the boat, emerging minutes later with more blankets under her arm, determinedly swinging the cool box. Smoothing out rugs well clear of the water's edge, she lifted the lid on her treasure trove—ice-cold drinks, together with fat green olives and the sweet dates she'd found in Saif's galley. 'I told you I could be useful,' she said when he complimented her on the spread.

They ate in silence, but at least it wasn't a hostile silence. It was more of a rebalancing exercise, Antonia concluded.

'What are you doing now?' he demanded as she stared up at the moon.

His voice made her tingle, made her want to stretch out

her hands to feel the cooling surf on her racing pulse. She concluded it was best to tell him the truth—or at least an edited version of it. 'I was just thinking I've had quite a day, what with the pirate attack, swimming through a storm and now you.'

'I see your point,' he agreed dryly, but just when she'd been sure they were making real progress he sprang up and walked away.

He had to put distance between them. It had been a long time since he had wanted a woman so badly. In fact, he couldn't remember wanting anyone as much as this girl. It was the ambience, he reasoned, pausing at the water's edge. There was nothing like a desert night to stir the senses.

He shook his head with amusement when she called, 'Wait for me!'

Nothing fazed her. And he wanted to wait for her, which prompted the question: when was the last time he had waited for anyone? 'I'm going for a swim, Tuesday—you stay here.' He dipped into the traditional Sinnebalese salutation before wheeling away. But the image of her nibbling dates with her small white teeth was still with him.

She was still feasting on the dates when she caught up with him. There was no artifice about her. She was hungry; they were on a beach, and she was eating to fill her stomach and not to impress him with finicky ways. She had a healthy appetite. He refused to dwell on that thought any longer than was necessary.

'Sorry,' she gulped, wiping her mouth with the back of her hand. 'You really shouldn't swim so soon after eating, Saif.'

She was giving him advice now? 'Is that so? And what

do you think you are doing now?' She was staring at the sky and waving her arms around, doing some sort of dance he found both innocent and seductive.

'I'm invoking the moon.'

'Of course you are,' he agreed wryly. 'And why are you doing that?'

'Don't laugh at me, Saif. For all you know, I'm a hand-maiden of the moon.'

'And I'm a camel. *Man jadda wajad wa man zara'a hasad.*'

'Oh, that's lovely!' she exclaimed. 'What does it mean?'

His gaze slipped to her lips as she repeated the words after him in Sinnebalese. 'He who perseveres finds,' he translated. 'And he who sows harvests—'

'Perfect,' she interrupted dreamily. 'It could have been written for me.'

'Then you'd better remember it, and I'll test you tomorrow.'

'Tomorrow?' Her face lit up and then became carefully expressionless again.

'We won't be sailing any time soon,' he confirmed, glancing at the sky.

'Great!' she exclaimed. 'Lots more time to dance.'

That wasn't exactly what he had in mind. 'You're crazy.'

As was the surge of desire he felt. She might be younger than him, but she warmed him with her *joie de vivre*, and it was hard not to smile at her antics. She drew him to her as no one ever had before, and he wasn't fighting it. Instead of wanting solitary time alone in the sea, he wanted Tuesday. 'Have you ever caught a fish?' he said, guessing that was a challenge she would find hard to refuse.

'I'd go hungry if I had to.'

The closest she had ever come to catching a fish was lifting one out of the freezer, Antonia realised.

'Would you like me to show you how to catch one?' Saif suggested.

She was so surprised by his offer she made the mistake of holding his gaze, only to feel her hormones riot in response. 'I'd like that.' The chance to do anything with Saif was an exciting prospect. And if she had to catch a fish…

She had not expected Saif to stand so close behind her in the rock pool, or to place his hand over hers when she plied the line. The fish were plentiful in the shallows, but all she could think about was Saif's warmth infusing her, and it was no time at all before there was a fish on the line and a world of erotic thoughts in her head.

This time Saif wielded the knife while she found fresh wood to make the fire blaze. They both took a hand in the cooking, and when Saif glanced at her and smiled it felt like all her Christmases had come at once. She could get things right if she believed in herself enough, Antonia concluded. A life of pampering didn't mean she lacked fibre— she just hadn't been tested before. Perhaps they were both finding out about themselves, she mused as Saif's glance warmed her. They weren't exactly friends, but they were certainly easier around each other, and there was something else that sprang between them, like electricity—something that made her heart thunder. 'What?' she said, angling her chin when he stared at her.

'I was just wondering about you.'

Wondering what? She blushed. If he was wondering if she was good in bed, he was in for the wrong kind of surprise. She was an amateur, a tease—a virgin, pretty much. It was better they direct their conversations towards harmless things, like business. 'The appointment I told you about?' she said brightly to distract him. 'That's not the only reason I'm travelling to Sinnebar.'

Saif's gaze sharpened.

'I'm here to find out about my mother,' she admitted, careful not to let her feelings show. 'She died when I was a baby and I learned recently that she spent some time in Sinnebar. How about you?' she prompted.

'Me?' He shrugged. 'This is just a break from work for me.'

'That's great. I can't think of anywhere better to relax.'

'I think it's time to swim,' he said, as if he was as keen as she was not to delve too deep. 'Unless you've seen enough water for today?'

'No, I like swimming.' Did she sound too keen? She was already on her feet. 'It must be way past half an hour since we ate,' she agreed, turning serious.

'Way past,' Saif agreed dryly, striding ahead of her into the foam.

CHAPTER FIVE

THEY swam like dolphins, and in spite of everything that had happened that day Antonia wondered if a day had ever ended so well. Saif was a much stronger swimmer than she was, and when a giant wave crashed over her head he was there in moments, drawing her to him where she felt safe. She was intensely aware of the brush of his hard, warm body against her own.

She felt safe and yet at the same time in the worst danger of her life, if only because no one had ever made her feel so aware of her physical self before. Saif made her want to swim better and to tease him all she could. She wanted to show off and flirt with him—with danger. Some small inexperienced part of her hoped he wouldn't notice her attempt to attract him, but the rest of her most definitely hoped that he would.

She would wait a long time for another night like this. They were miles away from anywhere on a desert island, with no one to see them as they stepped out of their normal lives and did whatever they wanted to do; they could be whoever they wanted to be…

And she wanted to be attractive to Saif.

She plunged into the waves at his side and began

powering out to sea, leaving him with no alternative but to go after her. Seizing hold of her, he trod water, demanding, 'What do you think you're doing?'

Her answer was to playfully spray a mouthful of salt water in his face. Astonishment barely covered it. He gave her a look. She dodged out of his grip and started swimming away. 'Last time I was too gentle with you!' he exclaimed, catching up with her again.

Her answer this time was to splash him as she called out, 'If you don't like it, catch me and punish me.'

And, like a sleek young otter she slipped out of his grasp and swam away again.

'Okay, I'm sorry!' She shrieked with excitement when he caught hold of her. She was playing with him as if they were lovers. But this was the Gulf, and he was a king, while she was…wonderful. She felt so warm and supple beneath his hands, and it was impossible not to notice that they fit together perfectly when he struck out for shore.

'You're not a bit sorry,' he accused, rejoicing in her defiance.

'Okay, not that sorry,' she agreed, her lips curving in a mischievous smile as she turned her head to look at him.

'Do you always live so dangerously, Tuesday?' he demanded as he matched his stroke to hers. This was shifting rapidly from surreal to erotic, he realised as he waited for her reply.

'Never as dangerously as this,' she admitted.

He could believe it.

'Anything rather than live a dull life,' she declared, putting her head down and diving into the waves as she used the power of the sea to drive her into shore.

There was nothing dull about her. She had more verve than his entire court put together. In a few short hours she had pointed out what was missing in his council of elders— personality, youth and vigour were just a few of the qualities he could name. And however passionate he was about taking Sinnebar forward he couldn't steer each new initiative himself. It would be good to have someone like her on board, he thought fleetingly, before dismissing the idea as ridiculous. But she was young and vital, and though she made mistakes in many ways Tuesday was a kindred spirit. How could he blame her for getting things wrong, when the only people who never made a mistake were those who never tried anything new?

'Can't you slow down?' she begged him finally. 'I'm exhausted pretending I can keep up with you.'

He laughed and called back some taunting challenge, but slowed his pace and waited for her. He was already standing, well within his depth when she swam past him. Her safety was paramount to him and he rode shotgun behind her as she waded into shore. She was strong in mind and in body, and he could understand how she had escaped the pirates, but did he need the complication of such a high spirited young woman in his life? The answer to that was a firm no.

Building a case against Tuesday was easy, he concluded as she turned to smile at him over her shoulder—another point in her favour, he conceded wryly. She would challenge him. She would prove more than a match for most men.

But most men couldn't have her.

He was suffering a bad case of desert-island fever, he decided, determined to put her out of his mind.

'Where are you going, Saif?' she demanded, catching hold of his arm when he turned to walk away from her.

As she stared into his eyes he felt tugged right in, as if Tuesday's eyes held the secret of life. 'Isn't there enough sand to go round?' He pretended impatience as he stared at the vast stretch of beach turned silver by the moonlight. 'Must we inhabit the same square metre of sand?'

'That's up to you,' she said.

He held her gaze. Her eyelashes were clogged with water and her lips were slightly parted and moist. She was excited at the thought of what might happen next, while he knew only too well he could offer her none of the things she dreamed about.

Nor would he stand by while she heaped more reasons for regret on top of what had already been a traumatic day for her, he determined, pulling away. But then he knew this was the opportunity he had been looking for to ask Tuesday a question that had been nagging at the back of his mind. If she had been assaulted during the attack, he would call ahead and arrange specialist counselling for when she returned to the mainland.

Saif's question should have embarrassed her, but it didn't. They had past that marker some time ago, Antonia realised, and now she owed him the truth. 'The boat was attacked,' she explained, 'But I jumped into the sea before they could touch me.'

'Bad enough,' Saif commented.

And it could have been so much worse; they communed silently in a moment of real contact between them.

Then, incredibly, Saif's eyes warmed as he stared down

at her, and his lips tugged in a slow grin. 'You came out of it well,' he said.

Time stood still as they stared at each other, while her heart pounded louder than the surf. It wasn't that Saif touched her—he didn't need to when she swayed towards him.

They were cool from the sea, but she was hot, hot enough to make the sea boil when he kissed her. He tasted salty and clean and wonderful, and her wildest fantasies could never have conjured up that hot-cold, salty-sweet kiss.

'Am I safe?' she murmured when he released her, without opening her eyes.

'You're as safe as you want to be,' Saif told her.

'Not safe at all, then.' Her lips started to curve in a smile as she looked at him.

'You're not frightened of me?' he said.

'A little,' she admitted.

He shook his head. 'How can the girl who swam through a storm in no visibility and no guarantee of success be frightened now?'

'Because I think you are a very dangerous man,' she told him softly.

'Hmm. Are you cold?' he demanded as she shivered with anticipation.

Her answer was a sigh, and so he nuzzled her neck, and everything inside her melted.

'You can always go back to the yacht and sleep safely in a bunk,' Saif murmured.

'Why would I do that?'

'I've no idea.'

And then he strode across the beach, holding her in his arms as if she weighed nothing, while she linked her hands behind his neck and snuggled her face against his chest. It was the easiest thing in the world to believe they belonged together, and that this was their island with no outside world to complicate things or muddy the water. There was no tomorrow here, no yesterday, there was only now, with the ocean lapping rhythmically on a sugar-sand shore, with a sickle moon and diamond stars to light their way. There was just one man, one woman.

There was only this…

'Still feeling safe?' he said.

She drew a fast breath as he ran the fingertips of one hand very lightly down her arm. This was madness, she registered as her heart beat wildly. She didn't even know Saif. She might have fantasised about such things happening, but had never imagined they would.

Saif continued to tease her with the lightest touch. It was a touch that carried the promise of so much more, and that was all it took to convince her that she was free to do as she liked here.

Free to enjoy sex with a complete stranger?

Why not? Antonia argued stubbornly with her inner voice. 'Do you believe in fate, Saif?'

'Maybe.'

'You do. I know you do,' she insisted. 'Just think about it—why am I here? Why did I swim to this particular island where you were moored up? We were meant to meet,' she said with certainty, holding Saif's brooding gaze.

'It was the closest port in a storm for both of us,' he said, injecting some realism into her thinking.

But she did feel the pull of kismet, and was sure Saif must feel it too. 'I'm not frightened of you,' she said. 'In fact…'

Saif shushed her, and as he looped his arms around her waist her body responded with indecent urgency. This wasn't some soft, office-bound male. Saif was a barbarian, raw and sexual, and there was steel behind that brooding stare.

He would be tuned to every desire she had ever dreamed of. He was the mate nature had chosen for her, she decided, choosing to ignore the voice in her head that said he was ruthless, and that Saif lived his life by very different rules. This would be a night to remember for the rest of her life. Saif wanted sex, and she did too. What was wrong with that? Now his lips were soft and persuasive on her mouth and on her neck.

While his stubble was sharp like a warning.

She was moist and hot. She was ready for him.

But was she ready for sex with a man as experienced and as exciting as Saif? Could she trust him? Could she trust him enough?

She was more frightened of her own inexperience than she was of Saif, Antonia realised; she was frightened she might disappoint him.

The silence deepened as he stared at her. They were both fiercely aroused, and he took pleasure in keeping her waiting. Meanwhile, his strength and heat were washing over her, and his expression said he would exceed every dream she'd ever had.

She softened against him, arching her back to encourage his hands to move lower, and she groaned with satisfaction when he cupped her buttocks. It only took the smallest adjustment to angle herself so she could feel the steel of his erection, to which he responded by pressing and releasing her against him, allowing her a hint of the pleasure to come.

But she wanted more than this. All thoughts of standing hesitantly on the brink, and of decisions yet to be made, had vanished. Her world comprised the throbbing hunger between her legs. There was nothing more. One night, she argued with her inner voice. She had to. She had never known such a primal instinct to mate with one man, or even known that she possessed such hunger. It was as if Saif had made her supremely conscious of her feminine power.

As if he sensed this confidence in her, he swung her into his arms again and carried her on board the yacht. When he laid her on the cushions beneath the stars, she felt one moment of anxiety, because now it seemed Saif was hesitating. 'Don't you want me?'

'I want you.'

His eyes were flecked with gold and amber, and as he stretched out at her side his mouth curved in a lazy smile. 'Do you know what happens when you play with fire?' he murmured, toying with a strand of her hair.

'I get burned?' she said hopefully.

He laughed, and then dragged her close to whisper all sorts of outrageous suggestions in her ear—words that carried such an erotic charge she would reach a conclusion without him if he didn't hurry to put his promises into practice.

Saif wielded an unusual power over her, Antonia realised as his hands warmed and controlled her. She should be aware of that—and be cautious. She didn't know him or what he was capable of, but then she hardly knew herself in this new guise of reckless heat. 'I want you,' she murmured, quickly forgetting her reservations when Saif moved over her.

'You've got me.' Impossibly attractive and indescribably

intimidating, he was experienced and she was not, and she was only now realising he had prepared her to the point where there could be no turning back. To the point where she felt a frantic need to welcome him inside her as nature, and Saif, intended.

'Patience,' he whispered when she moved urgently against him.

Her obedience was partially rewarded when he feathered kisses down her neck, while his hands worked more productively on even more sensitive areas. 'Calm,' he commanded as she fought for breath.

'How…?' She couldn't even speak.

'Easy for me.' His lips curved with amusement.

'That's so unfair,' she complained in a gasp.

'No doubt,' he agreed evenly. 'But everything I do is for your own good.'

She knew what was for her own good—and it wasn't patience!

Saif allowed her no respite from his teasing kisses on her breastbone, the swell of her breasts and on her belly, where her wet top was pushed back. But did he feel *anything*? Antonia wondered. How could anyone be so controlled, when she was composed entirely of sensation?

She strained towards him, wanting him to acknowledge her arousal, and gasped with relief when he made the lightest pass of his thumb against the swollen tip of her nipple before chafing each in turn with the utmost delicacy. 'You're teasing me,' she complained on another shuddering sigh.

'Am I?' he murmured.

'You know you are,' she accused him, feeling more excited than ever at the thought of what else Saif had in store for her. But still he was distanced and unmoved. 'Don't you feel anything?' she demanded, close to breaking point.

'Plenty. Believe me, I feel plenty.'

Then why wouldn't he rush things along?

'I know exactly what you want,' he said. A faint smile curved his mouth. 'Soon,' he murmured, kissing her brow chastely, as if he knew every wicked thought in her head.

'No,' she burst out. 'Now!'

Saif laughed as he brought her into firm contact with the thrust of his erection. 'Is that what you want?'

'You know it is.'

She was lost in an erotic haze, desperately seeking more contact, and hardly aware that Saif was lifting her top over her head. Her bra followed and was tossed aside, and now her breasts gleamed pale in the moonlight, while her nipples were dark, thrusting peaks that called for his attention. 'Take me,' she demanded, thrashing her head about on the cushions.

Saif continued to stare down at her with faint amusement. He refused to be hurried, and so she thrust her breasts towards him in deliberate provocation.

He chose the time, and when he dipped his head to suckle she was nearly delirious with relief. Now the zip on her shorts was undone. She wriggled frantically to be free of them, desperate to be naked against him. And now the smallest scrap of lace divided them. He ripped it off.

'If you stop now…' she warned him.

'Yes?' he said mildly.

'I'll never forgive you.'

Saif's cynical expression was fuel to her fire. 'Don't you dare stop now,' she warned him.

He murmured something provocative in his own language, but then he stilled and, cupping her face in his strong, warm hands, he kissed her so tenderly she felt tears spring to her eyes. 'This is more than sex for you, isn't it?' she said with wonder when he released her.

She wanted to hear Saif say he cared, Antonia realised, feeling a pain in her heart when he remained silent. 'Please say something,' she begged him.

'What's left to say?' he murmured, nudging one hard thigh between her legs.

CHAPTER SIX

HE HAD never met a woman like her. It even occurred to him that he might have met his match. She begged him, ordered him, demanded that he pleasure her, whilst all the time pummelling him when she wasn't scraping her small white teeth against his flesh for emphasis.

'Easy, tiger-woman,' he murmured, taking hold of her. 'This isn't a battleground—we're making love.'

Love?

This was sex, pure and simple, something they both wanted and needed, something that could only happen on a night like this—a night detached from reality, a night when they were both free to throw caution to the wind.

Antonia, meanwhile, was lost to reason. 'Oh, yes,' she gasped as Saif's lean fingers delicately parted her swollen lips. She was on the highest plateau of sensation and greedy for more. 'Please touch me there.' She should be shrinking from this man she hardly knew, not using him for pleasure. But Saif had opened a door and she had walked through, and now he was exposing her to his gaze in a way she could never have imagined feeling easy with—but she did. She'd had torrid thoughts for as long as she could remember, but had never put those thoughts into action. Now all she could say was, 'Please…Please…' when what she really meant was, *oh, yes, that's right…* and, *oh, yes, thank you…thank you…*

Easing her legs over his shoulders, Saif dipped his head to touch her with the tip of his tongue. She shuddered with delight, wondering how she was supposed to hold on—and then he increased the pressure. Was this a test? She had never wanted to fail a test quite so badly. Then he tasted her, and in that moment, that string of moments, she knew she had found the exquisite high point of her life. Saif had taken her to a realm she hadn't even known existed where he could order her pleasure with the skill of a maestro.

Governed entirely by raging hunger, she reached her goal and dissolved into a starburst of pleasure, her shuddering screams slicing through the sultry night. But it wasn't enough. Rather than slaking her hunger, Saif had woken a slumbering tiger, and now all she could think about was having him deep inside her so she could claim him for her own.

Losing control with Saif had laid her bare, Antonia realised when she quietened. He might not have taken her fully yet, but she had given him something that could never be recaptured—her trust. Saif had taken a girl and made her a woman, and now there could be no turning back.

Forgetfulness was one of the most valuable commodities for men who could afford anything, and, briefly, Tuesday would provide that. She was resting, but not for long, he suspected. He anticipated a long and deeply satisfying night, but for now he was content to let Tuesday set the pace, especially with the news from the palace still nagging at the back of his mind. Why, with so many rooms to survey and create inventories for, had they rung him tonight of all nights with the news that the treasure room of his father's concubine had been uncovered?

It certainly killed off Tuesday's romantic notion of some rosy destiny for them. Did he need a reminder of the rapaciousness of women? Did he need a reminder of that other woman on a night like this?

He should forget the past, shut it out of his mind, but when he stared at Tuesday he thought he understood his father's weakness perhaps for the first time. He understood, but could not excuse it. He was a very different man from his father, and had not pledged himself to a country and its people to be distracted by anyone. His father might have squandered his reputation, but, *ma sha'a allah*, there wasn't the remotest possibility that Ra'id al Maktabi would do the same.

'What are you doing?' he demanded as Tuesday, having stretched languorously, came to kneel before him. He wanted her, but not like this—not like a king with his mistress on her knees in front of him, waiting to serve.

'I wanted to repay you,' she said innocently.

He frowned. 'Explain...'

'The pleasure? I would have thought you knew,' she said, blushing.

He knew that she had never looked more beautiful, but the sight of her naked and proud and on her knees in front of him made his head pound. In that one innocent and provocative gesture, Tuesday had thrown him back into a world where sycophants knelt and equals stood at his side.

Springing up, he brought her in front of him. Embracing her, he kissed her hungrily, and by the time he released her she had forgotten the moment that could have gone so badly wrong for her. He knew then that she had been right to say this was more than a sexual encounter, but he would never admit it, because he had nothing to offer her.

But this was…sweet.

Holding Tuesday safe against his chest, he rested his face on her tangled hair and savoured the uncomplicated moment. This could be as straightforward as he wanted it to be, he reasoned. Taking hold of her hand, he kissed her palm, and, closing his eyes, he inhaled her innocent scent, as if the magic of the desert could make everything right.

Saif's touch made her arch against him. Hot flesh on hot flesh inflamed her past reason. 'Pleasure me,' she demanded, drunk on sensation, rubbing herself against him. She was completely lost in the fantasy of the desert and the dark stranger she had always known she would find there. She trembled uncontrollably as the hardness of Saif's muscle bore into her soft flesh, and she was impatient for him to move lower so he could satisfy her needs. 'Oh, please,' she begged him, bucking helplessly beneath his touch. 'I can't wait any longer.'

'You must wait,' he told her in a stern voice.

'I can't—' Her voice wavered.

'Tuesday,' he instructed sharply. 'You will wait.'

She held his gaze, and then he smiled at her as if he was pleased with her. She found his voice hypnotic and seductive, while his eyes carried the promise of pleasure and the certainty of danger. She exhaled shakily as he pressed her down into the cushions, and he held her there with little more than a compelling stare. She moaned in complaint when he held himself aloof, while all she could do was writhe helplessly in time to the insistent beat between her legs. 'I need…'

'I know what you need,' Saif assured her, taking fierce possession of her mouth.

Sensation surged through her. She pressed against him, feeling stronger than she had ever felt. Saif's desire empowered her, just as his planned delays infuriated her. Striking his back in frustration, she wondered how long she was supposed to wait. Her body was ready; he knew this and still he tormented her. But, as he kissed her, something happened. He kissed away the image of an experienced man and a much younger girl and replaced it with two lovers of equal standing, so that now there was only a man and a woman, and a desert moon shining over them like a beacon in the watchful sky.

He had awoken a whirlwind. He would never have believed it of the girl, though he should have known from the moment she boarded his boat that she was wilful, strong, and courageous in all areas—and that their first encounter had only hinted at the fires beneath. When it came to sex, she had stated her needs in the bluntest of language, and appeared utterly without self-consciousness. She had even tried to take hold of him, and, finding her tiny hand would barely encompass half of him, she had exclaimed with impatience and angled herself hungrily—and this before the last of the exquisite tremors had had a chance to subside after her first bout of pleasure at his hands.

Cupping her chin, he made her look at him so he could

be sure she knew what she was doing. Her eyes were still misty with desire and with passion, just as he had imagined them, but there was purpose there too. She had discovered physical love and was elemental in her need. Suddenly struck by a spear of jealousy, he demanded,

'Would you do this with any other man?'

'Are you mad?' she demanded fiercely. 'There could only ever be you.'

For her sake, he hoped that wasn't true.

A cry of triumph escaped Antonia's throat as Saif moved over her. This time he would take her. This time he would make her his. She had waited for this all her life, Antonia realised—this man, this moment. Whether Saif would admit it or not, he was part of her life now.

For a single night.

Could one night last a lifetime? It might have to, she accepted, seizing hold of his buttocks with fingers turned to steel. She drew her knees up and, with all the power of her sex, she urged him on.

Saif plundered her mouth while she sucked greedily on his tongue. He tasted ocean-fresh, pure, clean and strong, and with that all the spices of the east combined to seduce her senses. Every part of her was pressed against him and every part of her was keenly aware of him. That love-making came naturally to her was a revelation, and, feeling as safe as she did with Saif, made it perfect. She felt truly free for the first time in her life; free to be herself. There was only one jarring chord, which was the certainty that this level of harmony could only exist with one man.

He sank into hot, moist velvet. He was so much bigger than she was, he had intended to take it slowly, but she claimed him greedily, using her strong, young muscles to draw him in. He brushed her mouth and tasted her shock at this new sensation, and tasted her approval moments later. Withdrawing slowly, he plunged deeper still, while she sobbed her pleasure against his chest. 'More? You want more?' he prompted.

Her fingers closed around his buttocks. 'I want it all,' she assured him huskily.

Holding her wrists in a loose grip above her head, resting on the cushions, he made sure that was exactly what she got.

They made love all night and only drifted off to sleep in the quiet hours before dawn. She woke in time to see the waters of the Gulf glistening like a glass plate, with lilac fingers of light the only decoration. The waves were still, and seemed as content as she was, lying snug in Saif's arms to wait for the start of a new day.

But she wasn't content, because today everything must change, Antonia remembered. Today Saif might ask her name again and she must lie to him. She trusted him to take her back to the mainland, but when they arrived they would go their separate ways. Last night wasn't real, last night was a fantasy. They didn't know each other's names, jobs, lives, or even where they were from; they had no future, and there would be no togetherness ever again. The pain she felt at the thought of it was acute, the irony unbearable. If this was normal life, they wouldn't be facing the end, but the beginning; a beginning that might even lead to love. But as it was…

She could so easily fall in love with Saif, Antonia acknowledged, taking care not to wake him as she stirred, but loving each other wasn't an option for them. She still had a job to do—a job she was determined to finish, and to finish well. She couldn't settle for giving up now and going home. If anything, meeting Saif had only inspired her to do more, to achieve more.

'You're awake,' he said, shifting his powerful frame in lazy contentment.

'I'm sorry, I didn't mean to disturb you.' Or to do anything to hasten the day, Antonia thought wistfully.

'I want to be disturbed,' Saif assured her, drawing her close.

She shivered with desire at his touch and didn't have the heart to bring what must end soon to an abrupt finish now. 'You're dressed?' she said, tracing the lines of the top he must have tugged on some time during the night. He was wearing shorts too, she noticed.

'I had to go and check on the progress of the search,' he reminded her.

'Of course.' She relaxed. But even as they entered into this most normal of conversations she knew the spell was broken. The look in Saif's eyes had changed. He was already thinking about bringing the pirates to justice, which required a speedy return to the mainland.

He confirmed it, springing up and shrugging his massive shoulders. 'No time to waste,' he said, staring out to sea as if to assess the weather. 'Things look good.'

She had been expecting this, Antonia told herself firmly, but it didn't make the pain go away. It hurt to know the magic had vanished, only to be replaced by the cold chill of unease—something she must shake off when she had promised to help Saif in every way she could. 'I'll go below to freshen up and dress.'

She wondered if he even heard her as he began the process of preparing the yacht to sail.

Saif sailed with the total mastery with which he did everything else, and it would have been a pleasure watching him at the helm had Antonia not been dogged by the same dragging sense of dread. Of course things could never be the same again between them; she knew that. And of course she accepted the fact that everything must change when they reached the mainland. But the cloud hanging over her refused to budge. It was as if the same fate that had engineered their meeting now decreed that she must suffer for it.

She had been tested quite a few times on this trip and come through, she reasoned in an attempt to reassure herself.

But who knew if she could do it again?

Antonia looked at Saif, who obviously didn't share her concern. If anything, he seemed to have gained new purpose. It was as if with every nautical mile they travelled he was slowly changing back into the man he must really be.

They shared the rhythm of the sea beneath their feet and little else now, Antonia reflected. He didn't need her help to sail the yacht, he'd told her, and so she was consigned to the role of passenger, a chance acquaintance who was being given a lift to port on a fabulous racing-yacht. 'Is that Sinnebar?' she said excitedly, catching sight of a coastline. She already knew it was. What she'd really wanted when she asked the question was for Saif to connect with her one last time.

'Yes,' he said briefly, but his focus was all on the coast. They had sailed past the lighthouse guarding the entrance to the harbour before Saif spoke to her again. 'You'll have to get changed,' he said. 'And clean yourself up.'

In a phrase, Saif had turned her back into a much younger girl who needed his direction. 'You can use the hose to get rid of the salt,' he went on. 'And you'll find some robes under the bunk below. They'll be too big for you,' he added as he swung the wheel hard to line the giant yacht up with its berth, 'But you can't disembark in Sinnebar dressed like that.'

Like what? In a few words he had made her feel ashamed. What did he mean about the way she was dressed? She was dressed like someone who had escaped a pirate attack—the same way she had been dressed all the time they had been together. Had Saif even looked at her? Had he even realised what he'd said? He made her feel like a piece of flotsam that had washed up on his deck and now had to be swept away. She *had* hosed herself down with the fresh water, and she *had* tied her hair back. She'd done everything possible to make herself look respectable.

What Saif was actually saying, Antonia realised, was that she must never refer to what had happened on their desert island again. What they had shared had been great, but as far as Saif was concerned it was over now, and she was a potential embarrassment to him. 'I'll cover what I'm wearing with a blanket,' she offered. 'No one will expect me to be smartly dressed.' She was willing to show her respect for tradition in Sinnebar, but had no intention of making a bigger fool of herself than necessary by stumbling over some over-large robe when she disembarked.

Saif acknowledged this briefly. 'An ambulance will be waiting at the dock to take you straight to the Al Maktabi clinic for a check up,' he informed her, swooping by to complete some other task.

'Thank you,' she called to his disappearing back. 'I appreciate your concern,' she told the empty space.

It was a marvel to discover she could hold in tears for so long. But who knew what she could do? Antonia mused as she leaned over the prow while the yacht came in to dock. She had a feeling she was going to have to dig a lot deeper yet.

She was on her way down the companionway to get the blanket when Saif asked if she would do him a favour. 'Anything,' she called back, knowing this was no more than the truth.

'Take this down with you when you go, will you?' He'd lashed the wheel, and, peeling off his top, tossed it to her. She was determined to keep her gaze firmly averted from the body she loved—the body that had loved her so expertly.

'You'll find a cream robe hanging in what to you would be the front of the boat,' he told her.

'And you want me to bring it to you?' she asked. She caught the still-warm top he tossed to her, resisting the impulse to bring it to her face and drag in his scent.

'If you wouldn't mind?'

Then, like a spotlight on the star of a production, the sun caught him full on the chest and her mind went numb. She stared at Saif's tattoo. It occurred to her then that she hadn't seen him stripped to the waist in daylight—something that certainly put her moral code in question.

But right now her moral code wasn't uppermost in her mind. She had done her homework before setting out for Sinnebar, and knew what the tattoo over Saif's heart represented. The snarling lion with the sapphire tightly grasped between its paws was the ruling sheikh's insignia. Anyone could see the symbol online, where it was emblazoned on everything from the royal standard to the coin of His Imperial Majesty's realm. It was said that Sheikh Ra'id al Maktabi of Sinnebar—acknowledged as the most powerful ruler in the Gulf—had chosen the lion as his personal symbol to reflect the power he wielded. It was also rumoured in the wider world that the clarity of the cold, blue sapphire reflected Ra'id al Maktabi's calculating mind and his love-proof heart. So now it seemed that the man she had dreamed of falling in love with, the man she had had so brief an affair with, either had serious connections with or was closely related to a royal family reputed to have no finer feelings beyond the call of duty, which they took very seriously indeed.

Or…

Antonia didn't even dare to contemplate this last possibility.

'Are you feeling ill?' Saif demanded when she groaned.

She stared at him, wondering why she hadn't seen it before—the regal poise, the air of command, the confidence of kings. 'A little dizzy,' she confessed, turning her back on him before she gave herself away. 'Maybe I'm suffering from delayed sea-sickness.' It was a lie, and a weak one at that, but it was all she had.

'Well, take care as you go down the steps,' Saif advised. 'Sit down for a while. Put your head between your knees and take some deep breaths.'

It would take more than a few deep breaths to blank out what she'd seen.

But Saif couldn't be the ruling sheikh, Antonia decided. Where were his bodyguards, his attendants, his warships off the coast? It was time to stop panicking and start thinking clearly. With that tattoo, he must have some connection with the court, so that was good news. She might have a chance to ask him about her mother before she disembarked.

Nursing this little bud of hope, she went below. She couldn't pretend she wasn't excited by the chance to root around while Saif was busy up on deck. Who knew what she might find?

She found the cashmere blanket and not much else of interest. Saif's personal quarters were bare to the point of austerity. She found the robe exactly where he had said it would be, but, far from being some fabulous luxury garment that a ruling sheikh might wear, it was a simple cream linen *dishdash* of the type that could be purchased on any market stall.

That imagination of hers would get her into trouble one day, Antonia warned herself, collecting up a pair of traditional thonged sandals. There wasn't so much as a headdress, or a golden *agal* to hold that headdress in place, let alone a fancy robe. Saif was simply a patriot who chose to wear his leader's insignia over his heart. The fearsome ruling sheikh of Sinnebar, known to the world as the Sword of Vengeance, he was most definitely not.

CHAPTER SEVEN

ANTONIA was standing at Saif's side as he edged the giant yacht into its mooring at the marina in Sinnebar. She was covered from head to toe in the blanket. Her choice; her last defiant act. The ache in her chest at the thought of leaving him was so severe she felt physically sick. She hadn't expected parting from him to hurt like this, though neither of them had ever been under any illusion that their time together was anything more than a fantasy that would end the moment they docked. So she only had herself to blame for feeling this way, Antonia reflected as Saif called to the men on the shore to catch the ropes. Saif was her fantasy; she had never been his.

Grow up, Antonia told herself fiercely, biting back tears. Was this the girl who had set out from Rome with such determination? So, dealing with life outside the cocoon was sometimes tricky and often tough—get over it. She had that one day to remember, didn't she? And one day with Saif had turned out to be the best day of her life.

To avoid breaking down, she focused her mind on the stunning panorama beyond the harbour. Everything about Sinnebar gripped her. It was Saif's homeland, and a place where her mother had lived. So many impressions hit her at once: perhaps most significantly of all, the desert—stretching vast and silent beyond this billionaires' marina, as far as the eye could see.

The desert...

She felt a frisson of expectation just thinking about the desert. It had always been her dream to go beyond the silken veil and uncover the secrets there.

Well, she had the longed-for chance now, though it hardly seemed possible that she was staring up at jagged purple mountains, or the unfathomable desert. In the opposite direction were the gleaming white spires of an internationally renowned capital city. Immediately in front were low-lying white buildings. They lined the pristine dock, and all the paved areas were equally well maintained. Even the road was newly surfaced. There were colourful gardens and water displays, which she took to be a sure sign of wealth in the desert, and guessed that each entry point to Sinnebar would have similarly high standards so that the visitor's first impression could only be good.

She was a little surprised to see the number of security guards on duty, but then reasoned that it must be quite an event when one of the multi-million-dollar yachts came home to roost. If you had never seen a man like Saif climbing the yard arm to secure a sail, you would definitely want to add that to your scrapbook of memories. Saif had not yet put on his robe, and was balancing on what looked to Antonia like a narrow pole suspended at a dizzying height above the deck. She worried about him; she couldn't help herself. But he wasn't hers to worry about, she reminded herself, and some other woman would share his life.

She turned her face away so Saif couldn't see the distress in her eyes when he sprang down onto the deck. By the time he had taken the robe she was holding out for him and slipped it over his head, she was under control again. She wouldn't break down now, not now, not so close to the end of this journey. She turned her attention instead to the waiting ambulance, and noticed there was a low-slung limousine parked next to it. She guessed that was waiting for Saif.

Impressive.

So he was a wealthy man who drove around with blacked-out windows—so what? He could have been the lowliest member of the crew and she wouldn't have felt any different about him. Both vehicles were surrounded by security guards, but she'd be an important witness in the piracy trial, Antonia reasoned, so there would have to be precautions taken for her safety. She looked at Saif, who was greeting the paramedic. To her eyes Saif couldn't have looked more magnificent if he had been wearing the silken robes of her imagination. Even in plain linen he had the bearing of a king. It wasn't just that he was tall and imposing, or incredibly good-looking. He had such an easy manner—with everyone except her, she realised ruefully. She was apparently invisible now. In spite of everything she had so forcefully told herself, she yearned for a sign from Saif that said she meant something to him.

She would wait a long time for that, Antonia concluded as Saif brought the paramedic over to meet her. 'Take good care of the patient,' he said. 'She's had a rough time.'

As he spoke Saif didn't even glance at her, though the paramedic, a much older man, gave her a kindly smile, which she returned before bracing herself to disembark.

'*Kum shams ilha maghrib,*' Saif murmured as she passed within earshot.

'I'm sorry?' She didn't understand and turned to look at him for an explanation.

'Every sun has its sunset,' Saif translated, and for the briefest moment she thought she saw regret in his eyes.

That was his gift to her. Saif wanted her to know it had been a special time for him. It was the only gift she could ever want from him, just as leaving him without making a fuss would be her gift to him. 'You're right,' she said so that only Saif could hear. 'All good things must come to an end.'

And then, conscious that the paramedic was waiting for her, she left the yacht with her head held high.

As the limousine swept up to the steps of the palace he felt the return to reality more keenly than usual, but it altered nothing. The moment he stepped out of the limousine, he was changed. That was how it had to be. This was work. This was duty. This was his life.

The palace was set like a rose-pink moonstone on the golden shores of an aquamarine Gulf. It was an elegant marble paradise, where every luxury man could devise awaited him, and a fleet of servants was devoted to his every whim. He had never troubled to count the bedrooms, and doubted anyone ever had. Soon he would be making a gift of this towering edifice to his people, but until that time he called it home.

He strode inside, greeting people by name as they bowed to him, lifting them to their feet when they knelt in front of him. He loathed the deference some of his fellow sheikhs actively courted, and lived austerely considering his fabulous wealth. He valued all the treasures history had granted him, but he valued his people more.

He bathed and then clothed himself in the costume of power, adopting the shackles of responsibility with each new item. The heavy silk robe reminded him of the weight of duty, while the headdress spoke of the respect in which he held his country and its people. The golden *agal* holding that headdress in place was his badge of office, like the jewelled sash he wore at his waist. The sash carried his emblem, which he had personally designed as a representation of his pledge to Sinnebar. The rampant lion picked out in flashing jewels was a warning to anyone who threatened his land, and the cold, blue sapphire clutched in its claws was the heart he had given to his country and his people. On the day of his coronation, he had vowed that nothing would alter the pledge of that heart, or disturb the order he had returned to Sinnebar following his father's chaotic rule. That history had come back to haunt him in the form of a woman long dead, his despised stepmother Helena, something he intended to deal with without delay.

While he was away it appeared a letter had been found in Helena's room. Written before her death to an elderly maidservant, it contained a photograph of Helena holding a tiny baby girl in her arms. That was why they had called him back so urgently. Trusted advisors could be relied upon to keep this revelation under wraps, but not for long in a palace so heavily populated it was almost like a city in its own right.

The baby wasn't even his father's child, but the Italian Ruggiero's, and should have had no entitlement to land in Sinnebar. But when Helena had died the land had passed in equal part to her children. His father had paid her off, because Helena was the mother of his son. Razi ruled his own country and had returned the land to Sinnebar. Helena's daughter had not. It enraged him beyond belief to think that a woman long dead, a woman who had brought so much grief to his family while she was alive, could reach out even now from the grave to threaten his land.

He shouldn't be surprised to find his father had left him one last problem to overcome, Ra'id reflected grimly, checking his royal regalia before leaving the room. They had never seen eye to eye on matters of duty versus the heart.

He left the robing room with a purposeful stride, mentally preparing for the task ahead of him. The prospect of encountering anything connected to Helena was distasteful to him. It was an excursion into a world he had no wish to go to. Helena's heir should be clearing out her belongings, but the identity of the baby in the photograph had not yet been established. He would read through the documents and see what he could glean. At least it should prove a distraction, he conceded grimly, for a man tormented by the memory of a dancing girl invoking the moon, as he listened in vain for the sound of her voice.

He would never forget his desert-island castaway, Ra'id realised as he paused to admire the elegance of one of the inner courtyards. With its mellow fountains and counterpoint of singing birds, it was possible to hope that there were enough distractions here in Sinnebar, so that in time her voice would fade and her face would slip out of focus, until one day she would be just The Girl—a memory consigned to history along with all the rest. Closing his eyes, he inhaled deeply, breathing in the heavy perfumes of the

East, waiting for them to blank out the girl's fresh, clean scent. When that didn't happen, he frowned and turned away. The courtyard, with its fretwork screens and carved stone palisades, was made for the type of romance he had no time for. He didn't even know why he'd stopped here.

His robes rustled expensively as he strode away, the sound of them reminding him at all times of duty. When he reached his office he would read the letter again and study the land deeds. He would not tolerate part of Sinnebar being casually handed over to someone who cared nothing for the land of his birth and who didn't even live in Sinnebar. He would soon put an end to this outrageous claim and bury Helena's legacy of turmoil once and for all.

Before transferring Antonia to a luxury hotel, they had advised her to stay in a private clinic for several days, to check for concussion. She'd wanted to say she'd had a blow to the heart, not to the head, but the nurses and staff had been so friendly, and she had welcomed the chance to rest and regroup in such a clean and efficient place.

Her bills were covered, the staff had explained when she'd started to fret about expenses. She'd had no need to ask by whom, Antonia reflected, wandering out onto the balcony of the luxury hotel suite where she had just been transferred to. All of this had been paid for by Saif. It had to be Saif. Who else knew she was here?

Knowing Saif had paid for her care did nothing to ease Antonia's heartache. The fact that he hadn't tried to contact her once only rubbed salt in a wound she doubted would ever heal. How could it heal when there was no cure for her feelings for Saif?

The light of another day was fading, coating the city in a honeyed glow. The pink marble walls of the palace were tinted a deeper red as the sun drooped wearily towards the horizon. Leaning over the cool stone balustrade, Antonia pictured her mother catching sight of this same palace for the first time. Surely Helena must have seen the palace? It was impossible to miss the magnificent building on a visit to Sinnebar's capital, where the palace dominated the cityscape.

Knowing so little about her mother, Antonia could only guess that she was following in Helena's footsteps. She had to believe that whatever she found in Sinnebar would bring them closer in some small way. She wanted to understand her mother's early life. She knew that Helena had been very young when she had come to the Gulf, so it was easy to work out that she had probably been a student, back-packing her way across the world. Having discovered this beautiful desert kingdom, she hadn't found the will to leave. It would be easy to give your heart to a country where gilded cupolas and cream minarets stood proudly against a vivid electric-blue sky, Antonia mused. She thought the vista over the elegant city squares to the palace beyond was the most astonishing sight she had ever seen.

The second-most astonishing sight, Antonia amended, remembering the moment a sexy brigand had confronted her on board his yacht.

She must forget Saif, Antonia told herself firmly, staring at the palace again. She had work to do, and must devote herself to that. The hotel housekeeper had explained that the palace she could see was now called the Ra'id al Maktabi palace, after their new leader. The woman had ex-citedly gone on to confide that Ra'id al Maktabi's stated aim was to bring Sinnebar into the twenty-first century, which included equal rights for women for the first time in the country's history.

Antonia hadn't failed to notice how the woman's face had lit up when she spoke of the ruling sheikh, and had gathered that the hopes of the people were invested in their new leader. No wonder Saif had been offended when she had teased him about his sheikh. She understood now that Ra'id al Maktabi was looked upon as the saviour of his country.

Before he could deal with the Helena problem, he wanted to make sure that arrangements for the girl's safe passage home had been made. The sooner she went, the better. Reports on her progress were brought to him daily, which made it impossible to close that chapter until she was gone.

He rang his secretary to check that everything was in place, and, having been reassured that all the travel details were in order, he was reminded of an appointment that evening, a charity event he must attend. It was an event in the old style with no women present. He was in the process of putting an end to this segregation of the sexes, before any more good brains were wasted—a thought that immediately brought a flashback of a very determined young woman. What would Tuesday make of an event where she wouldn't be allowed past the door?

There was a smile on his lips as he shook his head at the thought of her reaction, but the event was for charity, and had been organised during his father's reign, so he would make time for it. Whatever his personal feelings, he could put up with one more evening of wall-to-wall men. When he returned from the event he would set about reclaiming the land that had been stolen from his people, and would be relentless in his pursuit of the missing heir.

She wasn't going to waste a second regretting things that couldn't be changed, Antonia decided as she came in from the balcony to her sumptuous hotel room. Everything was so beautiful in Sinnebar; how could she not be filled with a sense of optimism? And what else could life throw at her? She had to be over the worst now.

In fact, she was feeling quite positive, if only because this evening had provided her with an unexpected chance to put her plans for the charity into action. Her official appointment at the palace wasn't for three weeks yet, and she had intended to use that time to travel the country and learn more about the people. But fate had presented her with an unrepeatable opportunity to get a preview of the movers and shakers in Sinnebar. The moment the girl at the reception desk in the hotel had told her there was going to be a charity event that evening in the hotel ballroom, Antonia knew she must be there. She didn't have an invitation, because no one knew she was in the country yet, but there was nothing to stop her slipping into the crowded ballroom and mingling. At least she had to try. All the local officials were expected to attend, including the ruling sheikh.

The ruling sheikh!

The thought of seeing him both terrified and excited her. The Sword of Vengeance—who wouldn't be excited? And her heart rate soared to think that Saif might be there too. If he was a close supporter of the sheikh, surely there was a very good chance?

Society events were second nature to her, thanks to her

brother's high-powered life. She would blend in and get to know as many people as she could, taking the first steps towards making her dream of becoming an effective member of Rigo's charity team a reality. At last here was something she understood and couldn't make a mess of.

There was a shopping mall at the hotel where Antonia found everything she would need for the evening ahead. She chose a simple silk gown in apricot silk and teamed it with a pair of flesh-coloured high-heeled sandals, and a beaded clutch bag in the same soft shade. The girl in the hairdresser's suggested a fresh orchid to pin in her hair as a finishing touch.

Understated and discreet, Antonia thought as she took a twirl in front of the mirror in her room. The gown had a floating chiffon throw to cover her arms, and her back was covered too, so the dress was modest. It was a dream of a dress, she thought happily as she left the room, with nothing about it that could offend in this most conservative of desert kingdoms. No wonder she felt so optimistic about the evening ahead.

CHAPTER EIGHT

IT WAS an all-male gathering, which was definitely not what Antonia had bargained for. She was rocked back on her heels and hesitated outside the ornately carved double doors. She quickly gathered, from the glances she was attracting from the security guards, that she would not be welcome inside the ballroom. But they couldn't stop her peeping inside the room. It was an exclusive occasion, judging by the number of ribbons and orders worn by the robed men already seated at the beautifully dressed tables. Crystal glass and silver cutlery glittered in the muted candlelight, and there was a buzz of anticipation in the hall, but absolutely no chance to slip in unnoticed as she had hoped. She would stick out like a sore thumb as the only woman present.

This was definitely not a suitable forum in which to lobby support for her plan, Antonia concluded. She had no option but to wait another three weeks for her official appointment. But, as she drew back in disappointment from the door, her heart wouldn't allow her to leave. What if Saif was coming? What if he was already here? *What if she could see him one last time?*

She couldn't leave, so she came up with a risky plan. She would try to get in at the back of the ballroom, where she could see some steps leading up to a mezzanine area. She would be able to see everything from there.

Including the man who sat on the sapphire throne…

Antonia's gaze lingered. She'd seen images of Sheikh Ra'id's sapphire throne on the Internet, but nothing could have prepared her for the actual brilliance of the gold, or the lustre of the royal-blue sapphires with which it was so lavishly studded. Just thinking about the man who would occupy this legendary seat of power sent a shiver down her spine. You crossed the ruling Sheikh of Sinnebar at your peril, she had heard.

Dragging her gaze away from the blazing splendour of this formidable leader's throne, she crossed the lobby and slipped out of the building. Skirting the perimeter until she found a side entrance, she waited until the security guards were briefly distracted and then slipped inside through the staff entrance. Shoes in hand, she pelted up the back stairs, feeling certain her heart would explode with guilty fear.

Fortunately, the door to the mezzanine level was unlocked.

More tables had been set out for dinner on this upper level, for less important folk, she guessed. Taking quick stock of the situation, she decided if she hid behind a pillar no one would see her, while she could see everything that was happening below. This was her chance to weigh up the type of people she would be dealing with for the charity, and even the slimmest chance of seeing Saif made it worth the risk. The thought of seeing him and the fearsome Sword of Vengeance all in the same day made her heart thunder.

Taking a moment to calm down, she studied her surroundings carefully. She was at eye level with the royal standard, which was suspended behind the jewelled throne. That image made her heart leap when she remembered the last time she had seen it had been on Saif's naked chest. That was all the prompt she needed to begin scouring the rows of tables in search of him.

He wasn't there. She didn't really need to look to know, her heart would have told her if Saif had been close by. She was still trembling with emotion and disappointment when a noise like a wave breaking on the shore swept over the vast auditorium. As everyone rose to their feet, Antonia held her breath, realising the ruling sheikh was about to enter.

There was a peal of trumpets and then a procession began. A group of older men all dressed in elegant ivory robes walked proudly down the broad aisle between the tables. As all the other men bowed low to them, she realised that each of them must be a king in his own right, which was a reminder of the power their sheikh wielded.

As this group fanned out to take their places around their leader's throne, Antonia strained forward, still hoping for a glimpse of Saif. Once again, she was disappointed. He definitely wasn't amongst Ra'id al Maktabi's attendants— and probably wasn't even a member of the court, she thought, angry with herself for allowing her imagination to run away with her. There was certainly no one to compare with Saif here.

She was distracted and missed the moment when the ruling sheikh entered the room. She didn't see him, but she felt his presence. It was as if the room had suddenly been infused with greatness, and yet he had entered without a fanfare. He had no need of one, she realised when she saw the ruler of Sinnebar for the first time. She could only see him from the back, but even so, as Ra'id al Maktabi walked towards the platform with the easy loping stride of a panther, she thought him the most imposing figure she had ever seen.

At last here was a man to compare with Saif, Antonia decided. Dressed in robes of deepest blue, the ruling sheikh was easily the tallest man in the room, and far more powerfully built than any other man. She was transfixed by him, and couldn't wait to see his face, but just as he was about to turn the gold *agal* securing his headdress flashed in the light and she was momentarily blinded. It was then they seized her from behind.

This wasn't quite how she'd imagined spending the evening, Antonia reflected miserably, having made herself as comfortable as was possible in a dank, cold cell with very little light and no heating. She had asked for a blanket and they had brought her a thin, scratchy one, which was probably all she deserved. What her brother would make of this latest exploit, she had no idea. She had pleaded for the right to make a phone call to him, and had given the guard his number, but had no way of knowing if the guard would act on her behalf—no way of knowing if she would ever be released. Curling up into a ball, she covered herself as best she could and resigned herself to a long, dark night of fear and uncertainty.

She must have dropped off, Antonia realised when she was awoken by a crash of arms. Moments later her cell door was flung open and light streamed in. By this time she was huddled fearfully in the furthest corner of the wooden bench that passed for her bed.

'Stand up,' a guard shouted at her rudely.

She did so and stood trembling with her back pressed against the wall, expecting the worst. She was both surprised and relieved when the guard backed out of the cell, though that barely left enough room for the man who entered next.

She felt a sting of disappointment. What had she expected—the ruler of Sinnebar ducking his head to enter her cell? The ruling sheikh with his jewelled belt? Or perhaps Saif, her desert prince, the dark stranger of her dreams?

For the first time in her life, Antonia resented her over-active imagination. It was always tricking her into expect-ing the best.

The best?

The man facing her now in his smart suit couldn't have looked more disdainfully at her if he'd tried. 'I can confirm the identity of the prisoner,' he told the guard, ignoring Antonia completely.

'Please,' Antonia said as the man turned to go. 'Please don't leave me here.' She sounded so pathetic, but she was desperate. 'I have to get a message to my brother in Rome.'

The man paused and then turned to her. 'Nigel Clough, Foreign Office,' he said, making no attempt to shake her hand. 'I'm standing in for my colleague from Rome who is attending a charity function tonight. You're lucky that someone with influence has arranged for your immediate departure from the country.'

Antonia gasped. 'Do you mean I'm being deported?'

'I wouldn't quibble if I were you,' Nigel Clough warned her. 'Just take the chance to go while you have it.' The man's pale gaze flickered disparagingly around the cell. 'Unless, of course, you have some plan to stay?'

'No, none.' Tears stung her eyes. 'Will you call my brother just in case it all goes wrong and they keep me here?' She handed over a screwed-up note on which she had written Rigo's private telephone number with a pen she'd accidentally borrowed from an unwary guard. 'Thank you,' she called after the starchy civil servant. Now she just had to hope it wouldn't be long before she saw the outside world again so she could pick up her life.

But they left the cell door open, and with a rush of relief Antonia realised the guards were waiting for her to leave. She had no idea what lay ahead of her, but one thing was certain— she wasn't staying here. Drawing the flimsy blanket tightly round her, she followed the guards along the same dismal corridors down which they had first brought her, and almost cried with relief when she stepped onto the street. Of course there was no imposing sheikh, or sardonic Saif, waiting to greet her. She shaded her eyes against the glare of an unforgiving sun. This was a sorry end to a brave adventure.

She flinched as the prison gates slammed behind her. She had survived a pirate attack and an assault on her heart, but she doubted she could survive her own self-loathing if she returned to Rome without a single one of her goals having been fulfilled.

Well, that was just too bad, wasn't it? Antonia admonished herself, bumping around in the back of an old army Jeep on her way to the airport. She had to bite the bullet and get on with life like everyone else. She'd got into this mess, and now it was up to her to get out of it. She'd go back to Rome, face up to her brother and prove both to Rigo and to herself that she was worthy of her brother's trust and that she could do what she had set out to do. This time neither pirates, guards, nor even a man who had carved his name into her heart would stand in her way

It felt like she'd hardly had time to unpack her suitcase before she was standing in an austere cubicle in a private clinic in Rome, getting dressed after her examination. Of course, it had been a little longer than that, weeks in fact, Antonia reflected. She felt she was enclosed in a stark white eggshell—white walls, white floor; even the curtain shielding her from view was white. But in the past five minutes since the doctor had confirmed she was pregnant her life had blazed with vivid colour. Yes, it had been an incredible shock to discover she was pregnant, but when the doctor had confirmed it her horizons exploded with possibility. This was so far beyond the bounds of anything she believed she deserved; she could hardly take it in. Except to say that having a baby both terrified her and made this the happiest day of her life.

She couldn't tell Rigo, of course. He definitely wouldn't understand—and he would certainly never trust her again. But she must tell Saif. It might not be easy to track him down, but it wouldn't be impossible when he had commanded such a notable yacht.

A baby, Antonia mused, leaving the clinic in a bubble of happiness that grew and grew. She was going to have Saif's baby. What better gift could he have given her than a baby she would lay down her life for, a child she would protect and nurture as a lioness protects its cub?

Ra'id's fist thundered down on the top of his highly polished desk. Was this possible? Could the girl he had lightly dubbed Tuesday be the missing heir? Had he been duped? Had he harboured a thief hiding behind the guise of innocence? Had the thief of his people's land been lying in the arms of their king?

Springing up, he paced the room. He could not reconcile the feelings of loss and longing he felt for the girl he had known as Tuesday with his very different feelings for the person he believed posed the biggest threat to his people's happiness. The whole point of lifting a country out of chaos was to unite all the warring factions and keep them focused on one common purpose, which was the growth and prosperity of Sinnebar—something he was determined would be enjoyed by all, whatever their position in life. To think of one vast strip of land being teased away, leaving families stranded on either side of it, was something he would not tolerate.

CHAPTER NINE

MAYBE it was only a few months in real time, but it felt like ten years of growing up had passed since the last time she'd flown over this turquoise sea on her way to the Gulf. At least on this occasion she was prepared, Antonia reflected, and full of determination to finish what she'd started. There would be no hitching lifts on fishing boats, or desert-island idylls—there would be no distractions at all. This time she was here on business with a track record of success behind her.

After returning home in disgrace she had cancelled her initial meeting in Sinnebar to give herself time to regroup. The wounds from her ordeal with the pirates had gradually faded, but not so the wounds in her heart, and her brother Rigo had taken some convincing before agreeing to give her a second chance. It was then Antonia had discovered that a broken heart was the best engine for change. To forget Saif, she had thrown herself into her work, and in a short space of time had managed to double the number of children they were able to help. Having picked herself up, she had gone on to open branches of her brother's charity in Europe. Sinnebar was the next natural choice, and it was a place she couldn't wait to visit, though negotiations at the highest level had been necessary to arrange a visa for someone who had been deported from the country.

But this wasn't all about work. While she was here she would find Saif and tell him about their baby. What would happen next was a little hazy at the moment, but she was sure they could come to a civilised arrangement.

She would succeed in achieving all her goals this time, Antonia determined. She had a child to protect and set an example for now—a miracle she was still getting used to. And expecting a child had only intensified Antonia's longing to know her mother. She was more determined than ever to find out what she could about Helena's life in Sinnebar. Finding Saif was perhaps the most important goal of all.

She'd settle for that, Antonia realised, tightening her grip on the briefcase that held all the paperwork relating to the charity. If anything, it was Saif who had given her the courage to continue this adventure, and just knowing she was in the same country as the man was enough to make her heart fly. She had a good feeling about this as she disembarked the aircraft.

He had watched her progress over the past three months, knowing she would come back to Sinnebar. She had no other option if she wanted to extend the reach of her brother's charity. Antonia Ruggiero, daughter of Helena Ruggiero; Tuesday; Wild-child; Criminal; Cheat.

Lover…

She had bewitched him once and would never be allowed to do so again.

He thanked the immigration official on the other end of the phone for informing him that the individual under surveillance had landed, and replaced the receiver in its nest. He would see Signorina Antonia Ruggiero at the meeting in his government offices this afternoon. Antonia had no idea he would be there. He would surprise her at her appointment with his Minister of Charities.

Had it been a chance meeting on his yacht three months ago? How likely was that? He would trust no one with Helena's blood in their veins, and the coincidence was too much for him to swallow. Antonia had come to Sinnebar, like her mother before her, to weigh up the ground before greedily scooping up whatever she could. No wonder she hadn't been prepared to tell him her name. The charity she represented might be wholly above board—he'd had it checked out—but as far as he was concerned Helena's heir was a cheat out to rob his people of their land. The reckless escapade on a local fishing-boat was nothing more than vanity for the indulged wild-child of an Italian industrialist with more money than sense. Antonia Ruggiero had set out to deceive him. She was a criminal with a plan to steal his people's land—a woman who thought she could stroll back into the country and threaten him with her mother's bequest.

Let her try. He was ready for her.

Ra'id smiled grimly as he buckled on his belt with the royal insignia emblazoned on it.

'Signorina Antonia Ruggiero,' a quietly spoken man announced.

As the double doors shut silently behind her, Antonia was instantly aware of an atmosphere of ceremony and history. She could see the majestic council-chamber with its high, vaulted ceiling had been adapted to modern life with consoles and monitors positioned in the centre of a highly polished oval table, but nothing could take away from the craftsmanship around her. The gilt scrolling on the ornate plasterwork, like the exquisitely tiled floor and the artefacts decorating the room, was magnificent. Life-sized murals on the walls picked out scenes from Sinnebar's past, while giant gold vases at least twice her height stood like sentries at the doors. The floor-to-ceiling windows allowed honeyed light to flood in, and the air was scented and streaked with sunbeams. She felt it was a privilege to be here where time was measured in millennia rather than minutes.

Air-conditioning cooled her as she walked deeper into the room, and as she drew close the dozen or so men seated round the table stood and gave her the traditional greeting.

'Gentlemen,' she said, dipping her head politely before taking her seat. She had dressed for the occasion in a sober, beautifully tailored suit, in a subtle shade of dove grey that was both comfortable and modest, and she was wearing hardly any make-up. Her hair was neatly tied back, and though she had already given one presentation that morning her enthusiasm for the charity project had kept her fresh and alert.

She had left that last meeting with a positive feeling. Many of the men the sheikh had chosen to sit on his council were family men and they had quickly come to share her passion for the concept. This meeting was the final stage before Sheikh al Maktabi put his seal of approval on the scheme. She had been assured he would, as the ruler of Sinnebar always put the interests of his people first. She fully expected to start work on a centre for parents and children to enjoy in the next few weeks—providing the ruling sheikh would allow her to use some of his land for the project.

He had to—he must—Antonia determined. Ra'id al Maktabi famously cared about his people. How could he refuse such a simple request?

She was halfway through her summing up when the huge, arched golden doors at the far end of the room swung open. She felt a shiver of prescience and, following everyone else's lead, she stood up.

The thought of finally meeting the formidable Sword of Vengeance was both a thrilling and terrifying moment for Antonia, but as she turned to catch her first glimpse of him the light streamed into her eyes. It made no difference. She could still sense his animal power as he strode towards her.

Tall and lithe, the ruler of Sinnebar was bearing down on her like a jungle cat, deep blue robes rustling rhythmically as he walked. At his waist a jewelled symbol flashed.

Fear rippled down Antonia's spine. She had imagined the infamous Sword of Vengeance would be older. Sheikh Ra'id al Maktabi of Sinnebar's reputation was built on the solid rock of dedicated service to his country, but she could see now that this was a man in the prime of life—and that for some reason he disapproved of her.

'Signorina Ruggiero.'

'Saif…'

The breath shot from Antonia's lungs as His Imperial Majesty, Sheikh Ra'id al Maktabi, clasped her hand Western-style in greeting. She would have known that grip anywhere, and the name Saif had escaped her lips before she'd had chance to think.

But now…

Antonia began to shake as a debilitating fear swept over her.

'Water,' she heard a man's voice command and then someone was drawing out a chair for her and she sank back. That same someone had stopped her falling, and now he settled her into the chair, and she found herself staring down the long stretch of table into the face of a man who was both a stranger and her lover.

And the father of her unborn child.

The realisation that the father of her baby was none other than the Sword of Vengeance was a devastating emotional blow. Most things she could get around, but not this.

Any hope she'd had of finding Saif and living happily ever after had just been crushed. How could she tell this man—this formidable king—that she was carrying the heir to his throne? When would she tell him? Would he be willing to grant her a private audience—or would he find out somehow and steal her child?

He was darker than night and twice as dangerous, she thought as Ra'id al Maktabi stared coldly down the table at her. He would think her a gold-digger, or worse, if she told him about the baby, and would almost certainly demand that any child of his would be brought up in Sinnebar.

At his signal the hiss of the air-conditioning was instantly subdued to a hum. 'Don't let me throw you off your stride, Signorina Ruggiero,' Saif—the man she must now think of as His Imperial Majesty, Sheikh Ra'id al Maktabi of Sinnebar—insisted evenly. 'Please continue.'

He made a gracious gesture with his hand, but she wasn't fooled. This was a man everyone obeyed on the instant or suffered the consequences—which would be swift and terrible, Antonia suspected.

Sipping the water they had given her, she tried desperately to collect her thoughts. It helped to think about the child inside her, the child who depended on her, and then she widened these thoughts to encompass the many children who were helped by the charity she represented, and who depended on her getting this right. 'Gentlemen,' she began, determined to pick up the discussion without too great a pause. 'I do have some spare proposals with me.' She turned to one of the ever-present servants at her elbow. 'Would you be good enough to hand this copy to His Majesty?' she asked politely, passing over a neatly bound folder of printed notes.

'You make a persuasive case, Signorina Ruggiero,' Ra'id concluded as he brought the meeting to a close. 'I will consult with my council, but I am persuaded to allow you to open a branch of your charity in Sinnebar.'

'There is one other point I'd like to bring up.'

The surprise around the table showed itself in a collective gasp. No one interrupted the ruling Sheikh of Sinnebar, Antonia suspected, but in this instance she had no option as there was one item on which the ruler of Sinnebar's agreement was essential. 'The land…' She got no further. No one, especially not Antonia, could have predicted Ra'id's reaction. Wily gazes dropped before the power of their sheikh. Ra'id al Maktabi hadn't even moved, but all the men around the table had detected some subtle change in him, and it was a change that threatened all of them—especially her, Antonia suspected.

But when he spoke Ra'id's voice was perfectly calm. 'We have a number of matters to discuss, Signorina Ruggiero,' he agreed pleasantly.

Was she the only person in the room to hear the edge of menace in that voice? Antonia wondered. But wasn't this the opportunity she'd been hoping for? She could tell Ra'id about their child. It might come as a bombshell to him, but she had to believe he would be as happy as she was when he got used to the idea.

Ra'id's smallest emphasis on the word *we* had been enough to dismiss the council, who rose as one and, having bowed low to their sheikh, acknowledged her briefly before leaving the room.

CHAPTER TEN

S HE was alone with Ra'id. Even the servants had vanished. Now there was just echoing silence and the most powerful man in the Gulf—a man whose unwavering gaze was now fixed on her. This was no susceptible lover who would be thrilled to hear about a baby, but a hard man of the desert—a warrior who would stop at nothing to protect his people, a man without the luxury of a heart. She would have to be honest with him. She would explain first about the charity, and when the business part of the meeting was over she would tell him her most important news. She had to draw on her courage and remember the meeting earlier that day. The men who reported to the sheikh had all been broadly in agreement with her plan—subject, of course, to their sheikh's approval.

But had she made herself clear enough to Ra'id? Antonia wondered when he continued to stare at her as if she had unwittingly committed some terrible sin. Opening her hands in appeal, she pressed on. 'It goes without saying that the charity will stand all the expense incurred in building this facility, and we'll be happy to pay the going rate for the land.'

'The going rate?'

His reaction terrified her. Springing to his feet, Ra'id cast a long shadow over the table as he leaned his balled up fists upon it. It was almost a relief when he straightened up and turned his back on her to walk some paces away.

But what had she done? She could not remember feeling quite so threatened, and any thought she might have had of talking about their child had vanished. In fact, glancing at the door, she realised her primary concern now was to protect her child from this man she didn't feel as if she knew at all.

'Where do you think you're going?'

She shrank back as Ra'id spun on his heels to confront her when she started collecting up her things. 'I can see it's not convenient for you to see me right now.'

'When will there be a better time?' he said, cutting her off at the door.

'Ra'id, please…' Tears were threatening, and she hated herself for the weakness, knowing this was a man who would not care to see her cry.

'Ra'id, please,' he mimicked cruelly. 'What is it this time, Tuesday? Are you here for a pay-off—or would you like a little more action first?'

'Ra'id, don't,' she begged, turning her face from his stinging scorn. 'I can't talk to you when you're like this. Please, let me go.'

'Not until we've discussed this land that seems to mean so much to you.' His voice was harsh and cruel, and his touch was unrelenting as he steered her back to the table. 'Sit down,' he said, indicating the seat next to his. 'You've seen this, of course?'

As she shakily sank onto the chair, he pushed a sheaf of documents in front of her. 'No. What are they?'

'I have copies,' he said, when she didn't even know what he was talking about.

She glanced at the title on the topmost sheet. 'I don't understand—this is a deed of land granted by your father to my mother.'

'Well done,' he said derisively. 'One of your best performances to date. You almost have me fooled.'

Antonia shook her head in bewilderment. 'I'm trying to make sense of this. I'm sorry if I'm not as quick as you...'

'Take your time.' His voice was full of disdain.

'You knew my mother?' Antonia glanced up in confusion, and then her gaze returned to her mother's name as if just reading it could somehow protect her.

'It would be hard for me not to know my father's concubine.'

'What?' The room began to spin. She had heard Ra'id, and yet her mind refused to accept what he'd said to her. Pushing her chair back, she stumbled awkwardly away from the table. 'I don't understand what you're saying,' she admitted in a voice turned dry and faint.

'You don't?' Ra'id's hard face mirrored his disbelief. 'Let me stop your performance before you get started. And understand this, Antonia—I have no interest in learning how dear your mother was to you, or how much you meant to each other—let alone how passionately she wanted you to have this land in Sinnebar.'

'Land?' Antonia demanded with amazement. 'What land?'

'Oh, please,' Ra'id said, shaking his head. 'Can't you

do better than that? You will never rise from the ranks of the chorus to become a full-blown leading lady if you can't put on a better act.'

'This is no act,' she protested, feeling as if a vice were closing around her chest. 'I had no idea my mother even knew your father, let alone that she was his mistress.'

'That's a polite name for it.'

'Stop, Ra'id—please, stop it!' Holding out her hand as if to fend him off, she willed him to stop heaping insults on top of the confusion inside her. Then it occurred to her that as her heart had just been ripped in two he couldn't do any more harm.

She returned quietly to the table where she sat down and scrutinised the documents. She had inherited land in Sinnebar and a property from her mother. She couldn't have been more surprised. The news that Helena had been the late sheikh's mistress on top of this…

But Ra'id gave her no chance to recover. 'Do you still pretend you know nothing of this?'

'Nothing—I swear.' It was hard to take in the facts. Not only had her young mother been the late sheikh's mistress, but Helena had been paid off when the sheikh had tired of her with this gift of land. It was clear the late sheikh had thought nothing of this valuable gift of territory within Sinnebar, while Ra'id viewed it quite differently. Ra'id was the highly principled conservator of a kingdom and guardian of his people, and no greater sin could have been committed as far as he was concerned. She could understand his resentment. She had inherited a parcel of his people's land. It was a gift that had been passed from Helena to Antonia, who was not the daughter of the late sheikh but Antonio Ruggiero, the man who had rescued her mother from this life of…

She had no idea what her mother's life had been like, Antonia realised with a sharp pang of regret. Raising her gaze to meet Ra'id's hard, uncompromising stare, she knew she'd get no pity from him. But he still dazzled her, unreachable as he was. He was like a dark force framed in light, and one she must soften if her proposal for the charity was to succeed.

'I will use the land for the good of your people,' she said, feeling her strength and her courage return as a plan began to take shape in her mind.

'You can only do that with my permission.'

'But you will—' She had sprung up too quickly, and now she was paying the price. 'You must,' she said weakly, clutching the table for support.

'Are you ill?' Ra'id demanded, observing her keenly.

'No, I'm not ill,' she managed, instantly protective of her baby. Ra'id's child was a royal baby and could be stolen away from her by the stroke of his pen. She had to be cautious now.

'A drink of water, perhaps?' he suggested.

Antonia nodded, glad of the reprieve, and also relieved that even in his darkest rage Ra'id still had some flicker of humanity left in him. She sucked in a deep, steadying breath as he poured some water for her. Pregnancy might have weakened her, but what it couldn't do was lessen her resolve, and she would not fail for want of defending herself against Ra'id's unfair accusations.

'This doesn't change anything,' he said, handing her the glass of water. 'You have your mother's blood in you.'

'As you have your father's,' she flashed back. Ra'id might frighten her, but she was no doormat to be insulted by anyone. She wouldn't give up, her gaze plainly told him; she didn't know how to. This was her last chance to find out about her mother, to build a branch of the charity here and make it thrive. 'It would be a tragic mistake if you allowed your feelings for me to impact negatively on what we can achieve together with the charity.'

His expression remained unchanged. It was as hostile as ever. It wouldn't be so easy this time to build a bridge between them, Antonia realised, but she was as determined to push her proposals for the charity through as she was determined that her child would know its mother. Ra'id might be all ruthless, barbaric force, while she only had a dream to sustain her, but she had a store of stubbornness she hadn't even begun to draw on yet. 'I'll need planning permission.'

'To do what?' he demanded.

'Having read through this document, I see there's an old fort on the land I have inherited.' Ignoring his darkening expression, she went on. 'I shall restore that.'

'So you persist in this fantasy?' he interrupted.

'Obviously I would consult you first where any changes were concerned,' Antonia rushed on, determined he would hear her.

'You should know the land your mother left you lacks its own water supply.'

She made the mistake of staring into his eyes in confusion, only to see that the mockery she expected was mixed with slumbering passion in his gaze. 'You're enjoying this,' she said faintly, shocked to think that Ra'id could still want to bed his prey when he was so obviously relishing this opportunity to destroy her.

'The water course is on the wrong side of your border—and, unfortunately, you have no access to it.'

'Unless you permit it?' she guessed.

'And I won't permit it.' Ra'id's dark gaze glittered with triumph.

'So my land is…?'

'Worthless,' Ra'id confirmed.

'But not to me,' Antonia insisted, remembering her plans. 'The land is not worthless to me.'

'Arid desert? What will you do with it—offer camel rides?'

'That's cruel and unnecessary, Ra'id, especially with the prospect of you opening a branch of my brother's charity here in Sinnebar.'

'Only if I head up the ruling council of that charity.'

'Is there anything you don't rule?'

There was one thing—or rather one person—Ra'id reflected as Antonia pursued her argument. He had forgotten how persistent she could be. How irritating.

How desirable…

He watched her closely, noticing how her gaze softened when she spotted some ancient artefact, or when she stared dreamily into the middle distance as she formulated her plan, only for that gaze to harden and grow anxious when he'd mentioned the drawbacks to the old fort she had inherited. Would she fight for it? Remembering the girl who had swum through a storm to reach land, he had no doubt she would. Although she could only find the idea of visiting an ancient citadel where her mother had spent her last few months in Sinnebar incarcerated intimidating, rather as if the ancient building had the potential to become Antonia's prison too.

She had not yet broken free from her safe cocoon at home, though she badly wanted to, he concluded. So what was holding her back? Was it him? Was she frightened of him? Or was Antonia more frightened by the secret she was hiding from him?

As if sensing the way his thoughts were turning, she met his gaze, and that briefest of stares told him all he needed to know.

When Ra'id took a step closer Antonia's throat closed, and her gaze fixed on the jewelled belt on his robe. The rampant lion worked in gold thread clutching a very large sapphire in its deadly paws was exactly as she had pictured it, and she though it a perfect illustration of his power. But she had a small child sheltering inside her, and was responsible for other children who couldn't help themselves. She had to ignore her own fears and press on. 'If the old fort is habitable, I could live there myself and supervise the renovations.'

'Are you mad?' Ra'id thundered.

Mad? Yes, and very frightened, at the thought of taking a baby into the desert—a baby who hadn't even been born yet. But if she turned around and went home she felt sure she would never be allowed back into Sinnebar and everything she had set out to achieve would fail. 'According to those documents you showed me, I am entitled—'

'You are entitled to nothing without my permission,' Ra'id assured her in a deadly quiet voice.

He was very close to her, and his intoxicating scent was scrambling her brain. She had to forget everything they had ever been to each other. Ra'id must know she hadn't changed or weakened just because he was a king, and that she was as determined as she had ever been to carry all her plans through. 'So the rule of law means nothing in Sinnebar?' she challenged boldly.

She might not have spoken for all the good it did her. 'I will pay you for the land,' Ra'id told her coolly. 'Money is no object. Name your price.'

Her body shook with a tremor of revulsion. 'I don't have a price,' she said fiercely, searching for some semblance of the man she had known in Ra'id's eyes.

'I will *buy* the land from you,' he explained as if he thought her mind had failed her.

'It isn't for sale.'

This was truly a man she didn't know, Antonia thought as Ra'id's eyes narrowed. This fearsome ruler of Sinnebar bore not the slightest resemblance to the tender lover she had spent one glorious day and night with three months ago. This man was hard and brutal, and he didn't have a heart—or, if he did, it was as cold as the gleaming sapphire on his belt. Ra'id al Maktabi was a warrior forged from steel; a man she considered had nothing to offer the child she already loved so deeply and completely. But, with a mission to complete, she could allow no time for sentiment. 'Before I leave for the property I have inherited,' she said firmly, 'I would like to see my mother's room.'

The silence crackled with tension as they faced each other. Both of them were rigid with resolve. Ra'id was clearly astonished that anyone would challenge his authority, while Antonia was equally determined not to back down. It was an impasse from which there seemed no escape until, to her surprise, a faint smile tugged at his lips.

'I see no reason why you should not be taken to see Helena's room,' he said.

'By you?' Antonia demanded, feeling her confidence seep away.

'Who better to show you round? I am more than happy to take you to see your mother's room,' he said. 'And tomorrow morning I will take you into the desert to see your land.'

Even as Antonia's eyes widened and her lips parted with surprise, she wondered why she felt so sure that the granting of a wish had never carried greater danger. It wasn't just the thought of taking her unborn child into dangerous territory, she realised, but the very real threat radiating from Ra'id. Then she reasoned that the desert was not an environment to enter lightly, especially now she was pregnant, and who better to guide her than Ra'id?

But if she hoped to soften him…

Hope springs eternal, Antonia remembered, gazing up into Ra'id's cold eyes. But he held the key to turning her dream for the charity into reality. The old fort could only live again with Ra'id's water supply, and that was one dream she wasn't letting go of. And how better to find the chance to tell him the news about their baby than spending time with him?

No, she had no option. If she was to have a chance of success she must be as committed to her purpose as Ra'id was to his.

'Your mother's room?' he prompted.

'I'm ready,' she said.

CHAPTER ELEVEN

HE COULD feel Antonia's suppressed excitement as he led the way down gilded corridors to the east wing of the palace, where the shutters had remained drawn for years, and the rooms were neglected and cast in shade. He could feel her fear and apprehension too. He could feel everything Antonia was feeling in the same unspoken transfer of energy he'd felt between them on the desert island, when he had been Saif and Antonia had gone by the name he'd given her. But there had been a change in Antonia since then. She had matured. She might have trembled at her first sight of him, but the flame of purpose had returned to her gaze. This wasn't the adolescent who had ransacked his yacht to claim her piece of bread and cheese, but a woman who would not easily be dismissed. Perhaps the sight of her mother's room would change that, he mused as they reached the door.

Antonia could hardly believe she was really here, within touching distance of her mother's room. It was hard to catch her breath when Ra'id halted outside the golden door. The workmanship on the jewel-studded panelling was more fabulous than anything she could have imagined.

'Is it real gold?' she asked naively as she admired the intricate workmanship.

'Everything you see that looks like gold is gold,' Ra'id informed her with no emotion in his voice. 'Shall we go in?'

'Oh, yes please!' she exclaimed, hardly daring to blink in case she missed anything. Her sense of anticipation was indescribable, and she put all thoughts of Ra'id knowing something she didn't—something unpleasant, maybe—out of her mind.

'Could we turn on a light?' she asked, hesitating on the threshold.

'Certainly.' Reaching past her, Ra'id switched on a cobweb-strewn chandelier. Even now he made her tingle, Antonia felt, touching her cheek as she walked deeper into the room.

Whatever she had expected after seeing that golden door, it was not this shadowy interior, with sheets draped over the furniture and dust motes floating in stagnant air. But what affected her most was the atmosphere of abandonment, she realised, slowly turning full circle. It was as if the walls were soaked through with loneliness and sadness. Her first impression was that this was not the happy nest of a pretty girl, but a prison, a cage—a gilded cage for the discarded mistress of a ruler who had tired of her and moved on. But her mother hadn't moved on, Antonia thought sadly as she trailed her fingertips across the yellowing cover of a fashion magazine. She thought that the saddest artefact of all. 'It doesn't look as if this room has been touched since my mother left for Italy,' she said, rallying determinedly as she turned to speak to Ra'id.

She thought he seemed surprised she was holding it

together. She raised an eyebrow, as if to say that nothing would shake her from her path—and that if anything this clearer picture of the young woman who had been her mother had only strengthened her resolve.

He watched her closely. Knowing Antonia's background, he had been half-expecting this indulged child of a fabulously wealthy father to cross straight to her mother's dressing table, where a tumble of priceless jewellery still lay in a careless heap. The valuable gems were awaiting collection and a detailed inventory by his team of assessors, and would have attracted most people's interest. But Antonia had stood in silence when she'd entered the room as if she were battling some emotion greater than he could grasp. It was an emotion that made her shudder and clamp her jaw so hard a muscle jumped in her cheek.

The seconds ticked by while both of them remained quite still, and then, instead of crossing to the dressing table, she went to the wall of windows and started sliding bolts back on the shutters. 'Can you help me?' she called to him, as if this was just an ordinary task. 'No need; I've done it,' she said, spinning round in triumph when he was halfway across the room. She opened every window to its fullest extent and light streamed in; with it came the warm, scented air. 'That's better!' she exclaimed, turning back to face the room.

She stood quite still for a moment and then proceeded to examine everything in orderly sequence. Having apparently satisfied herself, she made for the large double bed on its plinth in the centre, walking past the jewels flashing fire on the dressing table and on across the room. She ignored a silk gown glinting with rubies, that drooped sadly from a padded hanger, until she reached the bed, where she stared down for a moment until inch by inch she sank into a heap on the floor, as if the bones were slowly melting in her legs.

He was a hard man, who had made many hard decisions since taking the throne, and had seen many things in his lifetime that should have affected him but had left his factual mind largely untroubled. Yet when he saw Antonia weeping by her mother's bedside he had to turn and leave the room.

He was showing respect, Ra'id reasoned, leaning back against the door. He drew breath to steady his emotions, but however hard a face he turned to Antonia he could not stand by and see her broken. Her defiance was so much easier to deal with, he reasoned, knowing deep down he had hoped she would exclaim with pleasure when she saw all the pretty things in her mother's room. But instead she had got to the heart of the matter.

The heart of the matter…

Yes; the heart of the matter was the searing sense of loneliness and rejection Helena must have felt before Antonio Ruggiero had arrived and rescued her. He could see that now, thanks to Antonia.

But he could not hark back to a happier time on the desert island, because that was stolen time, time he still regretted. His life, every moment of his existence, was devoted to a country and its people, and that was where his duty lay; on that there could be no compromise. Antonia was not simply a girl he was attracted to, she was a threat to his people's future happiness, with those documents granting her land in Sinnebar. He would not allow chaos to return to his country. He would bury the past, whatever it took.

Pulling away from the door, he opened it and stepped inside the room again. Whatever he had expected it was not this—Antonia seated at the dressing table, calmly reading letters.

'Why didn't you tell me about these letters, Ra'id?' she asked him in a voice that was calmer than he might have expected.

Had he anticipated hysteria—a broken woman, crushed beneath the weight of grief? Had he forgotten the virago who had confronted him on the yacht with a knife? This was no girl to be easily dismissed, but a strong and determined woman, even if that woman resided in a young girl's body.

'I had no idea my mother even had a maidservant in whom she confided,' she said, flourishing the bundle of letters she'd found. 'No letters were ever forwarded to Rome.'

'That might be because your mother wrote to her maid-servant in English.'

'And the maidservant could only read Sinnebalese,' Antonia murmured, understanding. Then her face hard-ened. 'The maidservant might not have been able to read English, but she would have understood these.'

She was looking at photographs of herself as a baby in her mother's arms.

'I imagine so,' he agreed.

'You *imagine*?' Antonia bit out, springing to her feet. 'So why didn't I receive them?'

'They were overlooked, perhaps.' He made a dismissive gesture, but felt a surge of arousal as they confronted each other, both with passions raised. 'Are you finished here?' He held the door for her.

She shook her head slowly and her expression suggested she detested him. 'You have absolutely no heart, do you, Ra'id?'

He neither agreed nor disagreed with that assessment.

'I give up!' she flared. 'And don't think we're finished here.'

'You are finished here,' he told her coldly, pointing to the door.

She saw his shadow cross the courtyard from the window in her room and felt a pang of regret. Standing in her chaste, cotton pyjamas watching Ra'id stride purposefully towards some unknown destination, she realised he still had the power to take her breath away. If anything, the deep blue robes of office and the Arabian headdress, with its gleaming gold *agal* holding it in place, only added to Ra'id's menacing appeal. Though she had tried to hate him, that emotion was far too close to love. But how cold Ra'id had been when he'd looked at her, Antonia remembered; how dismissive.

And he was the father of her child...

As dusk thickened into glutinous night, she agonised over how to tell him. Was he visiting a lover now—perhaps some glamorous and frivolously dressed ladies in his harem? *The father of her baby.* The thought made her sick—sick and angry. Swallowing deep, she turned away.

Shutting the window to give the air-conditioning a chance to work, Antonia realised sleep was out of the question. How could she sleep with Ra'id in her head? But she had no rights over him; they were practically strangers, strangers who owed each other nothing, and who knew less about each other now than they ever had.

But she missed him, she realised, angrily biting back tears. And what would it bring her, this love of hers, other than distractions and more unhappiness? Antonia Ruggiero in love with the Sword of Vengeance? It sounded ridiculous even to her.

She padded barefoot across the room to her lonely bed. Some might think it generous of Ra'id to allow her to stay in such splendid accommodation, but she suspected it was his way of keeping her close so he would know what she was doing. He was orchestrating her every step, and what hurt the most was the knowledge that she was carrying his baby and couldn't tell him.

How much closer could they be than parents of a baby? Yet how much further apart? Antonia wondered, trailing her fingertips across crisp, white linen sheets on a bed she doubted she would spend even a moment on.

During the lonely vigil of the long night, Antonia considered what she had learned from looking through what remained of her mother's possessions. Helena had been very young, both in age and attitude, although she'd already had a son by the ruling sheikh when she'd moved to Rome to marry Antonia's father. Helena had never been allowed to see her son again. Poor Helena; a girl who had liked pop music and fashion, and who had traded on her looks, believing they were the key to happiness. She had discovered that in the end those looks were her downfall—for no one, especially not the ruling Sheikh of Sinnebar, had wanted beauty without substance when the novelty had worn off.

And, though Ra'id could never be called weak, he was his father's son, Antonia acknowledged, and that was the type of heartless individual she was dealing with. He couldn't even look at her without self-loathing, because she represented his one and only failing. Antonia was Ra'id's one breach of duty, and now she must be punished and driven away. Whatever was waiting for her at the fort, she suspected it was something Ra'id believed would end her quest once and for all and send her flying back to Rome in a panic. In one last act of cruelty, he was determined to be there to see her reaction for himself.

He drove his stallion hard. The horse was well-named Tonnerre, which meant thunder in French. When they galloped from yielding sand to a firmer path leading directly to the mountains, Tonnerre's hooves struck sparks off the moonlit track.

Then the horse smelled water and it took all Ra'id's riding skills to persuade the stallion to slow. When Ra'id mastered him, the stallion consented to walk, whinnying and snorting his disapproval. Ra'id loosened the reins, allowing Tonnerre to amble the last half-mile or so to cool him down.

When finally they reached the icy spring that emerged at the foot of the cliff, he sprang down, and, murmuring praise into one alert velvet ear, he removed Tonnerre's tack and allowed the horse to go free.

Free…

Something he would never be, Ra'id reflected as he leaned against cold, black granite watching his mount suck in water. He had chosen this path, though he would never be free from the ache in his heart. He thought of Antonia, asleep in bed, and had to wonder how one young girl could affect him so deeply. There was no future for them, and she was nothing but trouble. He had decided that the best course of action was to show her what awaited her in the desert, and then she would be pleased to go home, where he hoped she would fight some other cause.

Unwinding the black *howlis* from his face, he shrugged off his robe and dived into a pool turned frigid by snow-melt from the mountains. His last image before he sank deep was not that of a young girl sighing with passion in his arms but of an aircraft soaring into the flawless Arabian sky, as it carried Antonia and her foolish fantasies back to Rome.

By the time dawn peeped through the shutters, Antonia had drawn up a plan. She would use her own money to convert the citadel she had inherited without having to take anything from the charity's resources. She could only hope Ra'id might want to contribute his expertise and that of others around him to the project. Without their help, it could just be her best stab at an Arabian retreat, and she wanted it to be authentic down to the last detail. But before she could do any of that she must persuade Ra'id to give her the precious water supply.

She would have to appeal to his better nature and hope he had one, Antonia concluded, drying her hair after her shower. Startled by the sound of approaching hooves, she put down her brush and crossed to the window. Her apartment was on one of the highest floors of the palace, and she could see Ra'id returning to the stables. She knew it was him before she even focused on the man springing down from the ferocious-looking stallion. Even severe black robes only added to Ra'id's glittering majesty, but it was his barbaric vigour that had called to her before she saw him.

She shrank back. He stared directly at her. Could he feel

her too? It was as if he knew she was looking at him as surely as if she had called to him.

Pulling further back inside the room, she grabbed a steadying breath. She was right to think there was some invisible link between them, and wrong to believe it was fading when it had grown.

CHAPTER TWELVE

SO NEITHER of them had slept, Ra'id noted, carrying the image of Antonia's unusually pale face with him into his private quarters. There had been dark circles under her eyes and her face had been tense. Had she finally accepted there was no point in her staying on in Sinnebar? Would she return home without a fuss? And, if she did, how would that make him feel?

He showered fast before dressing in workmanlike robes, prior to striding at a brisk pace to the breakfast room where he had arranged to meet her. She was standing by the buffet table dressed in a safari suit, seeming uncertain while a manservant was doing his job well, trying to tempt her with morsels of food from the wide selection.

Everyone stood and bowed to him. Antonia looked troubled when she turned. 'Ra'id,' she said, causing a murmur of surprise by using his first name.

No one addressed him that way. In time he might have forgotten what his first name was, if it weren't for Antonia and his brother, he reflected wryly.

Desire for her swept over him as their gazes met and

held. But he had closed his heart to her, he reminded himself sternly, to protect her from a ruthless king.

'You had a good night, I trust?' he said, taking the plate out of her hands and choosing some delicacies for her himself.

'No. Did you?'

Would he ever get used to her bluntness? He saw hurt and disappointment mixed with the defiance in her eyes. She had expected him to come to her, he realised. However deep the rift between them, she thought they could get over it and pick up where they had left off. 'I rode out,' he said briskly. 'Is there anything else you want from here?' He scanned the buffet.

'No, thank you. Did you ride all night?' she asked innocently. 'Did you have things on your mind, Ra'id?' The look she gave him was fast and accusatory.

'No. Should I?'

She raised a faint smile. 'I guess not.'

Now her cheeks were flushed and her breath was coming faster, as if her heart couldn't keep pace with her emotions. He turned away, effectively dismissing her, but he carried with him her fresh, clean scent and innocent appearance. That and the appeal in her eyes had almost melted him, he realised, but thankfully he was ruled by his head and not his heart, so it was easy for him to walk away.

He had almost reached the door when he realised she was at his elbow. He glanced down. 'Yes?'

'I can't wait to see the citadel,' she said, as if this was a holiday for her and he was her tour guide.

He made a brief hum of acknowledgement, before sweeping on his way.

'What about your breakfast?' she demanded catching hold of his sleeve.

He looked down at her incredulously, ignoring the collective gasp.

She seemed unaware of it. 'Aren't you going to eat anything, Ra'id?'

His look hardened. 'I have more important things on my mind.'

'So you don't feel like eating either?' she said, actually tightening her fingers on his sleeve so the fabric was crushed.

'On the contrary—but I will eat in private.' He shook her off.

'Of course. I forgot,' she snapped. 'In your ivory tower.'

'Will you excuse me?' he murmured, ignoring the barb. Whether she would or not, he was going to the stables to make sure their horses were ready for them to leave at once.

She shouldn't have annoyed him. She ate breakfast, if only for the baby's sake, and returned to her room to get ready to leave. If Ra'id took her to see the citadel, which was by no means certain now, it would be no magnanimous concession on his part, but another opportunity to rub her nose in the fact that her dream of a fun-filled castle to be used to such good effect by the charity was a naive and frivolous plan. One which without Ra'id's water supply would fail utterly.

But she was going to call Ra'id's bluff. She refused to be put off by his threatening manner. She would go into the desert. Whatever it took she would find the water she needed somewhere, and then she would renovate the ancient building and make it live again.

The opportunity to tell Ra'id about their baby seemed

further away than ever, Antonia reflected anxiously, but she wouldn't get a chance to tell him unless she stayed close to him. She had to keep with her original plan to visit the citadel with Ra'id. How could she not when there was still this huge and pressing secret between them?

He watched Antonia stride across the stable yard in a blaze of purpose. She had put on a little weight, he noticed, and it suited her. She was glowing with health, in fact. Her hair in particular seemed to gleam more than it ever had, though she had made an attempt to tame the abundant locks in a severe chignon which did her no favours. The hairstyle was the one jarring note in her appearance—that and the look in her eyes.

So this was war, he thought with a mixture of anticipation and amusement. Excellent. Let battle commence.

'Are you ready to go?' she said, eyeing the quiet gelding he had chosen for her before raising an eyebrow when she viewed his stamping monster of a stallion.

He almost had to curb a smile at the sight of the girl he recognised even without a knife in her hand. This was Antonia white-lipped with determination, and even the kind gelding he had selected for her was hanging its head uncertainly, as if it sensed trouble approaching its back.

He soothed it with a gentle touch as she mounted up, and then said, 'Ready?'

Her gaze was like a lick of flame that wavered when he held it. Travelling into the desert with him wasn't so appealing, suddenly, he guessed. *On my own?* he imagined her thinking. *With you? Without anyone to take my part?*

'You have a hat, I hope?' he said. 'The sun is hot. You may have noticed?'

She crammed on the totally unsuitable headgear she had been holding crushed in her hand.

'That hat isn't suitable for the desert,' he pointed out.

'Well, it's what I'm wearing.' She gave the brim a defiant tug.

'You'll need this.'

She huffed contemptuously at the scarf he was holding out for her to wind about her face and head. 'Keep it!' she exclaimed, as if accepting anything from him was the first step on the road to damnation. 'I'm just fine as I am,' she assured him, wheeling her horse around.

One hour and a sandstorm later, she was begging him for the Arabian headgear.

'I suppose you think this is funny?' she demanded as he sipped cold, clean water from a ladle offered to him by the Bedouin who had set up temporary camp around a well of clean drinking-water.

'Not at all.' Having unwound the yards of fabric he wore to protect his head, neck and face, he was largely untroubled by grit and sand, while Antonia looked more like a sand sculpture, with her red-rimmed eyes the only sign that she was human. 'I have a solution for you.' He smiled.

'You do?' She glanced towards the stallion, where his saddlebags full of the supplies he considered necessary were hanging.

'Certainly,' he said, tipping the bucket of water over her head. 'That should clean you up a bit—and cool you down.'

Spluttering, she swore at him. 'Why, you—'

'Brute?' he supplied mildly, already on his way to retrieve the spare *howlis* he'd brought for her to wear.

By the time he had returned, the laughing women of the camp had helped Antonia to wash her hair, and were hustling her away between them, no doubt to find her something more suitable for the desert than her Hollywood gear. Bedouin were kind that way, he reflected; infinitely generous.

He waited with mounting impatience as the minutes ticked by, chatting with the men whilst keeping an eye on the women's tent where they had taken her. He wouldn't put it past Antonia to steal a camel and make a break for it—and this time when she left the country he wanted to be sure it was for good.

But as he held that thought Antonia just ducked her head to leave the tent, and now was coming towards him with her head held high and that seemingly irrepressible look of determination and challenge locked in her eyes. She was wearing a serviceable but undeniably sexy outfit. The Bedouin women knew a thing or two about such things. It comprised a robe and a headdress that both protected her and—regrettably, as far as he was concerned—made her seem only too well suited to the hostile environment. She didn't belong here, and in his opinion the sooner Antonia realised that, the better.

'Ready?' she said, taking her revenge cold as she sprang into the saddle of the gelding he was holding for her.

'Ready,' he confirmed, handing her the reins.

Far from buckling and demanding a helicopter out of what had to be both an alien and terrifying terrain for her, Antonia had adapted and was still intent on going forward.

So be it. He was equally determined that this would be Antonia's first and last taste of the desert adventure she so foolishly craved.

At least she was clean. The women had allowed her to use their private bath-house, which was basically a tent they had erected over the stream that bubbled up to the surface from some underground keep far below the surface. But never had a bathroom seemed more luxurious to her, or people more friendly and fun as they poured buckets of cold water over her.

It was the first time she had been able to relax in a long time, Antonia felt. The women had made that possible for her with their lighthearted banter and teasing looks through the tent flap, at Ra'id and then at her. She had tried to mime that he was way too important for her, and that anyway she wasn't interested, but they just laughed at her. And after an hour of constant teasing she found her hunger for Ra'id had only increased.

Black-hearted Ra'id, as she was determined to think of him, was already mounted when she stepped outside the tent. He was holding the reins of her horse with his gaze inscrutable behind the folds of his dark and forbidding headgear. Thankfully, the women had arranged her own scarf so that, just like Ra'id, only her eyes were showing—which meant he couldn't see her blazing cheeks, or the way her lips had swollen with desire for him. Perfect. She angled her head to give him a glare. She wanted to be sure he could see her resolve, and that she would go on with this without allowing any personal considerations to get in her way.

The fact that she was terrified—of Ra'id, of the desert,

of the safety of their unborn child—was something she, like countless women before her, would simply have to take in her stride. There was a job to be done, and only un-flinching determination was going to get her through it.

Antonia's heart sank as their horses slowed to a trot outside the crumbling walls of the ancient citadel. This was not what she had expected at all. Instead of a fine fort sitting foursquare in the desert, the fortress she had inherited from her mother was a sad, run-down place with doors hanging off the hinges and windows boarded up. 'No wonder you wanted me to see it,' she said to Ra'id brightly, determined he wouldn't see her alarm. 'It's a blank canvas, isn't it?' she said, making the derelict wreck sound like the most de-sirable real-estate on the face of the earth.

'It's a blank something,' he agreed.

It was just a pity her horizons had been stretched somewhat since arriving in Sinnebar so that now they encompassed doors formed from solid gold, decorated with gem-studded handles. And windows—always made of crystal glass.

She smiled to herself at the irony of it all and was glad of something to cheer her up as she stared at the dried-out skeleton of a once-majestic home. Shielding her eyes against the glare of a sky bleached white by the sun, she tried to sum up her decrepit inheritance. 'A heap of stones' was a generous description. 'Is it safe to go inside?' she asked Ra'id, who had reined in beside her.

'I'll take a look.'

Before she could stop him he had urged his stallion into a brisk canter and was almost instantly swallowed up inside the walls.

Sitting alone on a fidgeting horse, breathing air that was heavy and still, was an unnerving experience. The heat was like a smothering cloth that choked off the last of her optimism, and the silence was overwhelming. There was no birdsong here, no leaves rustling, no sound at all.

Patting her horse, she rested her cheek against the firm, warm neck for comfort. She had never felt the need of a friend more. Had her mother felt like this? Antonia wondered, imagining Helena's feelings on being moved from one palace to the next by her disenchanted lover. This ancient fortress must have come as quite a shock after the opulent palace in the city. Her gaze swept the pitted stone, lingering on the mean little windows. How oppressive a building could seem, she reflected, remembering Ra'id explaining on the ride that the old fort had originally been built as a defensive outpost to guard the nearby water-supply— water that would now be held from her at Ra'id's whim.

She was beginning to hate it here, Antonia realised as the minutes ticked by. The ancient citadel was like nothing she had imagined, and had nothing to offer other than a home to desert rats and scorpions. It was ugly, and it stood in lonely isolation in the fire-pit of the world. She must have been mad to think she could restore it. Surely no human being could bear to live in a place that was so remote and hostile? It was sheer vanity on Antonia's part to think she could wave a magic wand and transform this tumbling ruin into a welcome retreat for hard-pressed parents and their children. That was definitely a fantasy too far.

And where was Ra'id? She was growing increasingly anxious about him. Old buildings could be dangerous, and he had been gone a long while…

Antonia's imagination started running riot. If Ra'id came to harm because of her, she would never forgive herself—and how would she help him here? The sooner they left the better, she concluded, regretting her earlier optimism.

She exclaimed with relief as he rode into view.

'It's safe to come in,' he said, reining in his prancing stallion. 'Antonia?' he pressed when she hesitated. 'Have you changed your mind? I thought you were on fire to see this?'

When she saw the glint in Ra'id's eyes and realised this was a test, and that he expected her to turn tail and run back to the city as fast as she could, she said, 'I am keen.' And picked up the reins.

CHAPTER THIRTEEN

ANTONIA dismounted and led the pony into the cobbled courtyard. It was impossible to know what to expect once she went beyond the outer the walls of the old fortress, and she didn't want to risk the horse stumbling. She felt sick and weak with disappointment—although pregnancy might have had something to do with it, Antonia conceded worriedly, unscrewing the stopper on her flask.

As she drained the cooling water she was conscious of Ra'id watching her. Had he guessed? Did he know that she was pregnant? She really couldn't find the energy to fight him now; all her earlier defiance had drained away. It was one thing taking on a major building-project in the desert when she only had herself to worry about, but the baby meant more to her than anything else, and she hadn't realised just how hostile and isolated an environment this was.

She was defeated before she even got started. She wanted to go home. The old fort was a dreadful place; no one could possibly live here. No wonder Helena had been miserable. It must have been nothing short of torment for a young girl to be shut away in the desert.

Lashing her horse's reins to a rail, Antonia sank down on a hard stone mounting-block and put her head in her hands.

'Are you all right?'

She lifted her head. Ra'id sounded genuinely concerned.

'This isn't too much for you, is it?' he said.

'No, I'm fine,' she said stubbornly. 'But, unlike you, I'm not used to the heat.'

'It's much cooler inside the walls.'

As he spoke, Ra'id was unwinding the folds of his head-gear, slowly revealing his brutally handsome face. How could she have forgotten how the sight of him affected her? Antonia wondered, holding on to her composure by the slimmest of threads. 'Yes, it is,' she agreed, as if her heart wasn't pumping furiously at the sight of Ra'id so close, so hot, so masculine. 'In fact,' she added, determinedly, 'If there was only water on tap, this castle would be ideal for my purposes.'

'Then it's a pity you don't have water on tap,' Ra'id observed smoothly, reminding her never to be off her guard where he was concerned. 'Shall we?' he invited, gesturing towards the entrance to the living quarters in the old keep.

She was determined this would not be an emotional re-run of her visit to her mother's forgotten room, though she was deeply conscious of walking in her mother's footsteps as Ra'id led the way up the stone staircase to the main building.

This had to be the strangest experience she'd ever had, Antonia concluded. She was bursting with emotion at the thought of finally visiting the place where her mother had been exiled; finding out about her mother's past was something she had waited her whole life to see and understand. And here she was at last with the father of her child walking beside her. It should have been perfect. But this was the same man who wanted nothing more than to be rid of her. Where Ra'id was concerned she had a blind spot, Antonia admitted. She could never stop looking for a sign that he still felt something for her. *Keep looking*, she thought as they began the tour of dilapidated rooms.

How terrified Helena must have felt when she had arrived here a virtual prisoner, Antonia mused, discarded and exiled to the desert where she could cause no embarrassment to the ruling sheikh, parted from her child— could anything be more dreadful? And never knowing if she would ever see her little boy again. How must Helena have felt as she walked beneath this same cold, stone arch into an austere and forbidding citadel? A gift of land would hardly heal those wounds.

A glance at Ra'id made Antonia tremble inwardly. When Ra'id discovered she was pregnant, would he show her any more mercy than his father had shown her mother? The al Maktabis were warrior sheikhs, and Ra'id al Maktabi was the fiercest of them all. He thought the gift of this fortress and the land surrounding it had been a generous pay-off to her mother, but Antonia knew there were more important things than money and land. In her opinion there was nothing that could compensate for the crushing of a human spirit.

So what would she do if she were stranded here?

It was at that point, the same moment as they entered the dark and dismal building, that Antonia's empathy with her mother's situation began to waver, and she had to remind herself that Helena hadn't been as fortunate as Antonia, who had such strong support from a brother who adored her. It was easy to be strong when you had people behind you to give you confidence, Antonia reflected, knowing how lucky she was. And with that strength she would take a fresh look at the citadel, seeing the positive this time rather than the drawbacks. For instance, the small windows meant that the fortress would be cool by day, and she would make it even cooler by installing air-conditioning. The extensive terracing could be enjoyed in the cooler months, as well as at dawn and dusk, and if she took on the project she could even make it a practical memorial to her mother.

Would she take it on?

That all depended on Ra'id. Without his water, there was no project. She had to try the one thing that might touch him where she had failed. 'You've seen the photographs.'

Drawing to an abrupt halt in a shadowy rubbish-strewn hallway, Ra'id interrupted her. 'Photographs?'

'The photographs of the children our charity helps,' she said quietly. 'You saw the album during my presentation.'

'You can't seriously be thinking of bringing those children here?'

'Why not?'

'Do you want a list? And why would you even think of it when I have more palaces than I know what to do with going begging in the capital?'

'Because I want to do something, maybe? Because I don't want or need your handouts, Ra'id?' When his eyes narrowed with suspicion, her passion for the project overflowed. 'If you didn't expect me to make use of the fortress, why did you bring me here, Ra'id? Was it to teach me a lesson? Or to show me how inhospitable the place is so I will relinquish my claim on the land?' She found it impossible to keep the heat out of her voice.

'I thought you should see for yourself that your mother's legacy is nothing more than a meaningless sheet of paper—and if you weren't prepared to listen to me, then bringing you here was the only way I could make you see the truth.'

'The truth as *you* see it,' she returned hotly. 'You don't know me at all, Ra'id—though I can see how it would suit you to bring me here.'

'Suit me?'

'Yes.' She steadied herself by concentrating her thoughts on all those people who depended on her making a success of this visit. 'I think you pictured me taking a tearful look around before dejectedly mounting my pony and riding out of your life for good. Well, guess what, Ra'id? I'm not going anywhere. I'm going to stay right here.'

'And if you're deported a second time?'

Antonia firmed her jaw. 'If you do that, I'll shame you before the world.'

'You'd blackmail me?' Ra'id demanded incredulously.

'I'll do whatever it takes to see this project through.'

Now she knew she'd gone too far. She was alone with the Sword of Vengeance in the middle of the desert, where anyone could disappear without a trace...

'I suggest you consider very carefully what you say next,' Ra'id warned her in a voice that was all the more menacing for being low and calm.

Antonia held her ground, though she was trembling inside. Ra'id had to know she was no pushover, and that she would stand up to him, in this and in all the discussions to come—or else how could she speak up for her child?

There it was—the most important secret of all, glittering between them like the Grail. She could see Ra'id some time in the future, holding their baby, before handing the child back to her.

Was that wishful thinking?

The thought that it might be frightened her more than anything else. Surely they could come to a civilised arrangement where their baby was concerned? But was civilised even possible with Ra'id? This visit to the citadel where her mother had been incarcerated was bound to stir violent emotion in her, Antonia reasoned. But now she must control her feelings, concentrate on finding a way to touch Ra'id and convince him that her plan for the fortress would work if he would only agree to giving her the water she needed. If he agreed to do that, she could build the retreat for the charity, as well as a home and a purpose for herself and for her child.

'I understand why you think the worst of me.'

He looked at her with suspicion, wondering what this new, conciliatory tone heralded.

'But since the pirate attack,' she continued earnestly, 'my priorities have changed.'

His suspicions, already roused, grew. 'That's old news, Antonia. What's really on your mind?' He knew the answer to that question the moment Antonia's hands flashed across her stomach to protect it. *Antonia was pregnant?* 'Are you pregnant?' he asked her quietly.

'And what if I am?' she said defensively.

'Are you pregnant with my baby?'

'Do you really think there's any doubt?'

'How do I know?' Antonia's continued defiance in the

face of such momentous news drove him to explode. 'For all I know, you're like your mother in that respect too.'

If he'd thought the girl on his yacht a virago, this girl was a demon possessed. She launched herself at him. He captured her, holding her firmly in front of him. 'Think of the baby—if you can!' He was instantly aware of how it felt to hold Antonia, and was immediately remorseful for taking out his shock on the mother of his child. He let her go and stood back as she cried, 'There have been no other men, Ra'id—how could there be?'

This impassioned outburst revealed more than she wanted to say. 'Enough,' he told her softly. 'Do you want to upset yourself and the baby?'

'Upset?' Hugging herself, she turned away. 'Do you care about me now?' she demanded with disbelief.

If only she knew. He'd always known that one day he would face this dilemma: love or duty. But to him, with his father's history to draw on, there was no choice to be made. 'Of course I care about the child you carry. I have seen more grief than I care to think about brought down on a child thanks to the selfishness of its parents.'

'Don't tar me with that brush, Ra'id,' she warned him.

But as she confronted Ra'id Antonia knew that this was not one of her wild, romantic fantasies but a very dangerous situation. She had brought her unborn child into a desert kingdom where that child's father reigned supreme, and where its mother had no voice, no rights. She doubted Ra'id would let her go now he knew she was carrying his royal baby. What irony, Antonia thought as she stared up at the citadel's forbidding walls. She really was following in her mother's footsteps now. Would Ra'id make her a prisoner here like her mother before her? The loss of her freedom was a nightmare beyond imagining, and the very last thing she wanted for her child—but would Ra'id, a man driven so relentlessly by duty, respect that?

Ra'id would always do what was right, she concluded, but it didn't reassure her to know that he had accomplished many good things in Sinnebar without once involving his feelings. Plus, he had lashed out verbally at both their parents, whom Ra'id considered had failed his stringent test. With all his wealth and privilege, would Ra'id be so very different when it came to bringing up a child? For him, duty always came first. The only certainty, Antonia decided, was that she would never agree to be parted from her child, and neither duty nor self-interest would change that.

'You're going to live here?' The effects of pregnancy were more telling than he had realised, Ra'id concluded as Antonia stated her intention. 'Firstly, the place isn't habitable, and secondly, you would need my permission.'

'I can't do this without your help, Ra'id.'

'I'm well aware of that. But first I would have to agree to you remaining in the country.'

'Don't you want to keep your child in Sinnebar?' It was a passionate outburst in a last-ditch attempt to touch him. It was also the biggest risk she had ever taken in her life.

'I have a country to consider.' *And now a pregnant mistress*, Ra'id acknowledged tensely.

'And I would be superfluous to your plans?' Antonia suggested with biting accuracy. 'If you think for one moment you're going to part me from my child…'

He only had to picture Antonia staying in Sinnebar to know he still wanted her. And only had to think of his child to know he wouldn't let her go. But she represented everything he had pledged to avoid. The irony wasn't lost on him. Having shunned his late father's self-indulgent lifestyle, it now appeared that he was following his father's lead to the letter. Was he to lose everything he had fought for? Was the country he loved to be plunged back into chaos? Could he hide Antonia away as his father had hidden her mother? Just the thought of it disgusted him.

Would he pay her off when the child was born...?

Antonia might shun money now, but didn't they say everyone had their price? 'I won't part you from your child; I'll help you.'

'Thank you.' Her face softened and hope returned to her eyes.

'If only to ensure you do a proper job at the citadel.' His tone was brusque and businesslike as he struggled to remain immune to the Antonia effect.

'Oh, I will,' she assured him, her face transformed by happiness and wreathed in smiles. 'You have no idea how hard I'll work.'

'Not at the risk of your pregnancy,' he commanded.

'Of course not. I'll be sensible,' she promised him fervently.

'No more wild adventures.'

Only with you, flashed briefly across her eyes. 'None. I promise,' she said. And then she flung herself at him, hugging his unresponsive body, exclaiming, 'Thank you, thank you!'

There was such rapture on her face, and such vulnerability in her expression, while his mind was full of the fact that he was going to become a father—the very best of fathers—and he would be ruthless in achieving that end.

* * *

Thanks to the narrow windows it was surprisingly cool inside the many rooms, and far less threatening than Antonia had originally thought. In fact, now she was inside the citadel, it seemed to welcome her, though there would have to be some fairly major changes. During the renovations she would ask the architects to find a way to bring in more light and make the place seem more welcoming.

If only Ra'id could welcome her, Antonia thought wistfully as he accompanied her on the tour. But, of course, Ra'id was only doing this because she was expecting his baby. He probably wouldn't let her out of his sight now—but not for the reasons she had hoped. He might be walking at her side, but she was on her own—as her mother had been before her. Antonia was looking for a very different resolution. Her mother had wanted to escape, while Antonia was determined to stay. She wanted to bloom where she was planted and make a go of things here.

They had looked inside many rooms, but when Ra'id stopped outside a particular door she got the strangest feeling. 'This is my mother's room, isn't it?' she said, not really needing Ra'id to confirm that it was.

He said nothing as he opened the door onto what, at first sight, appeared to be yet another soulless, dusty room.

Antonia was determined to keep her emotions in check this time, but there wasn't a part of her that wasn't aware of Ra'id or a fragment of her heart that didn't yearn to have him close to her again. She missed the easy camaraderie they'd come to share on the island, when it had been just a girl called Tuesday and a man called Saif. But now there was a king and a girl who was nobody, except for the fact that she was expecting the king's child. She had value as the incubator of Ra'id's child, Antonia acknowledged, but equally she was a liability to him.

So she must plan for the future.

She stared around walls that seemed to beg her to linger so she could see the possibilities. 'I'd need some form of transport to get in and out of town,' she murmured out loud, thinking of all the shopping she would have to do to turn this place into a home.

He stared at her long and hard, and then he said briskly, 'A four-wheel drive should suffice. It isn't far to the city— and, of course, you'll have a full complement of staff. You can have a driver and a helicopter at your disposal, if you think that's necessary. I'm sure we can come to an accommodation that suits both of us equally.'

'An accommodation?' That sounded like a cold, soulless thing. And, as for suiting them both equally, she doubted Ra'id knew much about equality, and cared to learn about it even less. 'Will I be free to use the resources on my land?' She was thinking local wildlife, the flora and fauna, when Ra'id's expression darkened.

'Do you imagine you're going to find oil here?' he demanded.

'No, of course not, but I was hoping you might allow a number of specialists to advise me on the best way to showcase local wildlife and crafts.'

'I could make some enquiries when I return to the capital,' he conceded.

'When *you* return?' Antonia's courage dwindled to nothing, but then she firmed her resolve. Ra'id had never pretended they would be living anything other than separate lives; it was up to her to get used to it.

'I'll leave you to take a look around in private,' he said.

'No. Please stay.'

'As you wish. I'll open the shutters for you.'

As he did so the light streamed in, and she noticed something glinting so softly she almost missed it. Lying forgotten in the dust, a tiny necklace sparkled in the light. She scooped it up and slipped it into her pocket. It was a diamond-studded heart on a broken chain, and carried enough vibrations for her to know that it must have landed on the floor when someone had snatched it from their neck as they ran out of the room.

Her mother, maybe—tearing off the necklace before she'd left the citadel for good?

Ra'id remained silent in the background as she walked slowly round the room. It was impossible not to notice the many photographs, poignant reminders of a small boy with dark, curly hair and bronzed skin—a boy who looked a lot like Ra'id. 'So, this is my brother,' Antonia murmured, lifting up one of the frames to study the image more closely before carefully putting the frame back in its place.

'This room hasn't been touched since your mother left—in a hurry, I'm told.'

And who could blame her? Antonia thought, shivering as she remembered the tiny heart on its broken chain currently residing in her pocket. 'It seems unfair that anyone would accuse Helena of deserting her little boy.'

'What would you call it?' Ra'id demanded from his very different perspective. 'When she was heard crying out that Razi was the worst mistake she had ever made?'

'I would call this imprisonment,' Antonia said, gazing at the heavy door with its prominent lock and bolt. 'Maybe my mother was no longer attractive to your father once she'd had a baby—I don't know the reason. She was frightened and very young. But I do know Helena must have been distraught, losing her child, and she wouldn't have kept all these photographs around her if she hadn't loved her son.' Antonia's hand flew to her mouth as she stared around what to her seemed little better than a prison cell. 'I'm not surprised Helena seized the opportunity to escape.'

'And yet you want to live here?'

'I wouldn't be living here under duress.'

And she was a very different woman from her mother, Antonia realised, knowing all the fripperies of life she had previously thought so important to her had only left her hungry for real-life experience, like an unrelieved diet of canapés when what she longed for was steak and chips. 'And any time I want to leave, I'll just have to jump in the car…' The words froze on her lips as Ra'id stared at her, and somewhere deep inside her heart she felt a stab of panic.

CHAPTER FOURTEEN

HE LEFT her tidying her mother's room. He couldn't bring himself to stand over her, and any thought of gloating as Antonia viewed the sad trivia of a life given over to pleasure had vanished. Whether he cared to accept it or not, Antonia had made him see things differently. Helena had been a victim, and a very young victim at that, with no means of helping herself. He could see that now, and his father should have seen it years back, but it was too late to revisit the past and change the mistakes that had been made. Instead, he chose to do something about the present, which in this case meant getting down and dirty with the plumbing to see if it was possible to bring water here.

It would take major restoration work, he concluded, but it could be done. He found he was pleased about that as he closed the door on the ancient boiler-room and walked up the steps into the light. He was just brushing off his hands when he spotted Antonia heaving a sack out of the building. 'What do you think you're doing?' he said, racing across the courtyard to lift it out of her hands.

She squinted her eyes against the sun in order to stare

SUSAN STEPHENS

149

up at him. 'Collecting things for the thrift shop. You do have them in Sinnebar?'

'Yes, we do.' He gave himself a moment to rejig his air of command into something more accommodating for the mother of his child—a woman so determined to go ahead with her plan it wouldn't have surprised him to see Antonia with a spade, digging a trench to change the water course by herself, if she had to.

'You collect and I'll carry the bag for you,' he suggested, wishing he could remain immune to the fact that Antonia had obviously been crying. She'd put on a brave face for him while they had been in her mother's room, but the moment he had left it, she must have broken down. 'We'll stack them in here,' he said briskly, trying to harden his heart to her and failing miserably. 'I'll have everything collected and cleaned, and then distributed to the appropriate agencies.'

'So you do have a heart, Ra'id,' she said.

'I wouldn't go that far,' he said dryly, but he was relieved that Antonia was recovering. This visit couldn't have been easy for her, mentally strong as she was. So much for his determination not to get drawn in! He almost convinced himself that today was different, and that today he had no alternative other than to help her out; having agreed to help Antonia make the place habitable, he would delegate the work to the most appropriate team of experts the moment he returned to the capital, and at that time he would distance himself from her. 'Now, I think you should rest.' He was concerned for her, and worried that her enthusiasm for the project would make her forget that she needed to look after herself now.

'Rest? Rest where?' she said, gazing anxiously around the derelict ruin she had inherited.

Following her gaze, he felt her uncertainty, and her sense that the enormity of the task she had taken on might just be too much for her in her present condition.

Feeling nothing when she stared at him trustingly was a battle fought and quickly lost. 'I'm going to take you somewhere to rest up where you can bathe in fresh, clean water.'

'The water you'll be bringing here,' she said quickly, as if he might be allowed to forget.

'That's right,' he said, admitting to rueful admiration as he went to fetch her horse. 'The water you'll need if you're still interested in restoring this place?' He turned to look at her when he'd checked the girth.

'Still interested?' she demanded. 'You don't know me, Ra'id.'

But he was beginning to. This time she didn't pull away when he offered her a leg up onto her horse.

This just wasn't fair. Of all the things Ra'id had said or done, bringing her here was the cruelest—somewhere so beautiful, so tranquil, so instantly enthralling.

They rode the short distance in silence. She didn't know where Ra'id was taking her beyond his promise of rest and fresh water, but as they crested the dune and she saw his tented pavilion on the shore of the oasis she could have cried at the beauty of it—and with despair that this awe-inspiring wilderness she was quickly coming to love could never be hers to enjoy free of Ra'id's disapproval.

She felt gritty and grubby as she eased in the saddle to

survey the limpid and oh, so tempting waters of an oasis streaked with moonlight.

'What do you think?' Ra'id asked, reining in his prancing stallion beside her.

'I think it's the most beautiful place I've ever seen in my life,' she said honestly, starting the steep descent.

Leaning towards her, Ra'id steadied her horse. 'If you want to take a dip, I'll keep watch while you swim…to make sure you're safe.'

'You'd do that?'

'Of course,' he said, as if it were no big deal.

They had reached the flat ground, and Ra'id was waiting to help her down. 'I can manage, thank you,' she said, freeing her feet from the stirrups, but she was weary as she slid down from the saddle. She pulled herself round before facing him. The days of showing her soft underbelly to the world, and to Ra'id al Maktabi in particular, were well and truly over. 'Would you like me to light a campfire while you see to the horses?'

Ra'id unbuckled the saddlebags and threw them over his shoulder. 'If you're up to it.'

'I'm up to it.' She rested one hand on her horse's warm, steadfast neck for a moment, thankful for the survival course her brother had insisted she must take before involving herself in any more dangerous sports.

'Then let's set up camp.'

'Do we have food?'

He patted the saddlebags.

'You've thought of everything.'

Not quite. He had totally underestimated her, Ra'id concluded as Antonia walked ahead of him to the pavilion.

* * *

She wasn't quite out for the count, and had enough fizz left in her to agree when Ra'id offered to light the fire after she had helped him with the horses. 'You swim,' he said. 'Go on—you've earned it.'

She had nothing to prove, Antonia realised. She didn't have to stand on her pride, or work herself into the ground. They'd been a good team, and they could both cope with outdoor living, though Ra'id understood this terrain a lot better than she ever would, and he would know just where to look for tinder.

She couldn't see Ra'id when she reached the edge of the oasis, so she dropped her clothes and plunged naked into the water. The sudden chill on her overheated skin was like a healing balm, and as she powered into her first stroke she felt her cares float away. Everyone needed time out, Antonia reflected, rolling onto her back so she could stare up at the lantern moon. This precious time in the desert had been a welcome reminder that she could make a difference if she tried.

She would make a difference, Antonia determined, idly swishing her hands in the water to keep her afloat. Turning towards Ra'id's beautiful pavilion, she started swimming towards it. This was a scene that belonged in one of her fantasies, but if it had been she could have engineered a happy ending rather than this travesty: Ra'id and Antonia trapped in the middle of a drama of their own making, a drama that should have ended well before they made love…

But thank goodness it hadn't ended, Antonia reflected, caressing the still-flat planes of her stomach as she waded out of the water.

* * *

He watched Antonia until she was safely out of the water and dressed again, and then, without her seeing him, he returned to the campfire he had lit earlier. Should he show her what he had found in her mother's room? Was she ready for it, or had she suffered enough emotional upheaval for one day? Would it be better to throw it on the fire? While Antonia had been scooping something off the floor, he'd been too—something that had dropped off her mother's dressing table, another pathetic, hand-scribbled note.

'Ra'id!' Antonia exclaimed, drying her hair with a towel he'd laid out ready for her. 'You're cooking fish again.'

'In anticipation that you will fillet it for me again.'

'I might,' she said, her lips curving at the memory, though she hunkered down a good distance away from him. 'Of course I will!' she exclaimed now, as if some thought had suddenly occurred to her. 'If you promise I can have that water.'

'A filleted fish in exchange for my precious water-supply? Do you think I'm mad?' He might as well have added 'Do you never give up?' But he knew the answer to that already.

'Shake on it?' she said boldly.

He looked at the tiny hand stretched out to him, and just in time remembered how the desert affected him. It was another magical setting, where they could be anyone they wanted to be while they were here—the only difference now was they both knew there were consequences to embracing that freedom.

'You're smiling,' she said as he ate the morsels of fish she had prepared.

'Am I?' He frowned.

'What's wrong, Ra'id?'

He wasn't about to share his thoughts with her. He had concluded that the enemy to duty wasn't self-indulgence, but love. He wasn't sure he had the weapons to fight that enemy off. 'Why don't we have a swim?' he said, badly in need of a change of scene.

'It's too soon,' she cautioned him.

'Then we can stroll round the oasis, and when I judge the time is right I'll throw you in.'

She was off like a hare from the traps. 'Not if I see you first,' she called back to him, laughing.

They didn't make it to the water. The restrictions of the real world had been lifted again and nothing stood in their way. She was young, seductive and he wanted her.

She was fine until Ra'id brushed against her. He'd kicked sand over the fire and helped her clear everything away. She had identified the thick, nobbly palm-trunk behind which she intended to leave her clothes, and he was at the water's edge when something frightened her, a crawling thing…

A harmless lizard, Ra'id reassured her as it scuttled away.

'Okay, so I'll get used to them,' she said determinedly.

'If you intend staying in the desert, I'd definitely advise it.'

There was humour in Ra'id's voice and warmth in his eyes. She didn't imagine it. She had been hanging on for a sign that he would mellow so they could discuss the future together, and it turned out the desert had cast its spell over him again. In the capital he was the undisputed king, but the wilderness was a leveller that stripped everyone's position in life away. And Ra'id came out of that well…

Very well, Antonia reflected, feeling increasingly aroused as he continued to stare at her. There was so much strength in his dark gaze, so much wisdom and understanding of her needs.

'You're aroused,' he murmured.

'Am I?' she whispered, making it sound like a challenge.

'So aroused, if I touch you you'll come.'

She was too shocked to answer, by which time she was in his arms. He carried her into the pavilion and laid her down on the freshly laundered cushions. She was enveloped in the scent of sandalwood and sunlight as she sank into their scented folds. Moments later she was naked, and so was Ra'id; he had judged her level of arousal perfectly.

'You greedy girl,' he murmured as she abandoned herself to the onslaught of pleasure.

She was whimpering, open-mouthed in surprise that such levels of sensation were possible when he eased her legs over his shoulders. Being back with him was like a miracle, and so was the speed with which he could coax her into readiness again.

'Let me ride you!' she demanded, desperate to feel him deep inside her.

'You set the pace,' Ra'id agreed, settling back on the cushions.

She lowered herself cautiously. Ra'id was huge, and she had to take him in gradual stages. His touch was tantalisingly light on her hips as she sank slowly down. Then he was touching her, delicately, skilfully with one fingertip, and she was moving faster, with more confidence…wildly, and with abandon.

He turned her so fast she had no chance to protest—and why would she, when he was giving her exactly what she needed firm and fast?

Ra'id climaxed violently with her, and they clung to each other for minutes that turned into drowsy hours; two people, so close they were one.

'Do you ever tire?' she asked him a long time later.

'With you?' Ra'id gave her an amused glance. 'Never.'

This time he made love to her tenderly, as if he cherished her above all things. She wouldn't allow herself to believe that, of course. She knew it was some primal instinct at work that prompted a man to feel that way about the mother of his child. If she allowed herself to believe in his feelings for her, Ra'id really would possess the means to break her heart.

But he didn't make it easy for her. Brushing her hair back from her face, he moved slowly and deeply, kissing her eyelids, her lips and her neck, making love as if they had all the time in the world and he rejoiced in that as much as she did.

Dawn was busily brushing away the clouds of night when she woke in his arms. Would she ever become used to Ra'id's strength, or his beautiful body? Antonia wondered, snuggling close, determined to make the most of whatever time they had.

'So, you're awake,' he murmured.

'Just,' she admitted, loath to be the first one to break the spell.

'It can be like this always, Antonia. For you and me.'

'What do you mean?' She turned to look at him.

'We can be together,' Ra'id said, as if that were obvious.

'And the baby?'

'Of course the baby,' he exclaimed softly. 'We would be a family.'

She rested against him, thinking how wonderful that would be—how perfect. But life was never perfect. Ra'id was a king, and whatever plan he had brewing in his head she wanted to hear it before she agreed. 'Tell me more,' she said.

'Not now.' He smiled a slow, sexy smile. 'It will be a surprise.'

When had she learned to be such a pessimist? Antonia wondered, moving away. How much more did she want than this? Coming back to rest her head against Ra'id's naked chest, she inhaled his familiar scent, telling herself that nothing could be more perfect than this. She should be happy. She should be optimistic about the future.

So why wasn't she?

Because this was all an illusion, Antonia admitted; this wasn't right. Or, rather, she wasn't right for this. She wasn't her mother, and she wanted more than to be hidden away— the sheikh's plaything. She wanted a family. She wanted to work. She wanted to make a difference.

CHAPTER FIFTEEN

HE SENSED the change in Antonia and knew he would have to work hard to reassure her that his plan for her would work. His father had blanked out a son and had dumped his discarded mistress in the desert, but he would never do that. Freedom was as important to him as it was to Antonia, and was the bedrock of the constitution he had installed in Sinnebar. 'I'm going to take another swim,' he told her, 'While you can have your own private stream to yourself.' She smiled at him as he glanced towards the back of the tent where the luxurious bath-house was situated.

His life was nothing without Antonia's bright flame in it, Ra'id realised as he grabbed a towel and strode away. She consumed his every waking moment and invaded his dreams at night, filling him with hunger for her, as well as the absolute determination to keep her at his side.

She found what looked like a page from a diary underneath the robe Ra'id had worn the day before. She guessed he had found it in her mother's room at the fort and the sheet of paper must have fallen out of his pocket. Backing deeper into the pavilion, she began to read it.

She'd never tidy up again, Antonia determined, biting back tears. Like so many things at the fort, it must have been churned up, passed over and forgotten. She handled the single sheet of paper carefully, sniffing it, studying it, imagining her mother writing it, knowing it had been written in despair, and in hope that one day someone would read it.

I wanted everyone to know how I had to live in the last few years, so you would understand why I went to Rome.

It was a scrawled page that told of unbearable loneliness—of no one for Helena to talk to, or to share her fears with, and a child stolen away from her, a blow that no deed of land could ever soften.

Money, land and jewels, in however much abundance, had done nothing to ease a young girl's desolation, Antonia could see, and for a moment she felt numb. Then Antonia realised her main reaction to this page from her mother's diary was frustration, because it was too late for her to sort out her mother's life. She could only be glad her father had found Helena, and that they had been able to share a few months of happiness together before her mother's untimely death.

Realising she had scrunched the piece of paper in her hand, she carefully straightened it out again and put it with the other treasure she had found at the fort—the broken chain, with the tiny, diamond-studded heart. She would rather have these small things than all the riches in Ra'id's treasury, Antonia mused, because the broken heart and the note scrawled in the childish hand were in many ways her mother's true legacy. And if she didn't learn from them, she really would let her mother down, and the note would have been written for nothing.

Ra'id was with the horses when she came out of the tent with the intention of confronting him about her discovery. 'You've saddled up,' she said with surprise.

'I have something to do—for your benefit,' he assured her.

Ra'id was smiling, but she sensed that once again he was the autocratic ruler who had made some plan without consulting her. 'Don't I have any say in this?'

'You'll be quite safe here. Though you can't see them, there are security guards everywhere.'

'Oh, good…' That was supposed to make her feel reassured?

'Trust me—I'll be back within the hour.'

The gap between her belief they had grown closer and the true situation had just widened into a gulf, Antonia realised. She loved Ra'id and could never say no to him, but as she watched him ride away she thought that perhaps the time had come to do that.

No? Antonia had said *no* to his suggestions for her immediate future? They were in the pavilion, facing each other, and the atmosphere between them was as tense as it had ever been. He had offered her the sun, the earth and the moon, and Antonia had turned him down. 'I don't think you heard me,' he said as she stood with her back turned to him. 'I will have the fortress repaired and refurbished to your specifications. You will have your own palace in the capital, *and* I'll open a bank account for you with more money in it than you could ever spend. And you can spend that money on anything you want.'

'Subject to your approval?'

'Well, *obviously* I'll have a say in it!' he exclaimed impatiently.

'A *say* in it?' she echoed, spinning round. 'You'll choose. You'll pay. You'll install me in one of your fabulous palaces and visit me as and when you wish?'

There was no mention of their child, Antonia realised, hoping the terror didn't show in her eyes.

'I thought you wanted that?'

She did want to be with Ra'id, more than anything on earth, but not like this. If she agreed to his terms she was effectively giving over her life for Ra'id to control. He would hold the purse strings, the decision strings, and as he already held the strings to her heart that was one string too many. But how easy it would be to become dependent on him, a man so compelling and powerful; he exerted some hypnotic spell over her. It would be madness for her to fall under that spell, however much she wanted to. She must remain free to make her own decisions, even if sometimes she got it wrong. First off, she had to know his intentions regarding their baby so she could counter them if she had to. 'What about our child, Ra'id? Where will our baby live?'

For the first time since she'd known him, Ra'id's gaze flickered.

'No,' she repeated firmly, closing her fingers around her mother's note.

'You're being unreasonable, Antonia.'

'If it's unreasonable to defend my unborn child, then I am unreasonable,' she agreed.

'Defend the baby against me—its father?' he demanded incredulously.

'No, Ra'id, I'm defending our child against the past—a past that still seems to rule us both.'

'What are you saying, Antonia?'

'When were you going to show me this?' She produced the single sheet of handwritten despair that she had found by his robe-pocket and had the small satisfaction of seeing Ra'id reach inside his robe to check that it had gone.

'You took that from my pocket,' he accused her.

'No. It must have dropped out.'

Dragging off his *howlis*, he tossed it aside. 'I picked it up at the fort and intended waiting until you had recovered before showing it to you.'

'Recovered?' she said with only the smallest shake in her voice to betray her feelings. 'Let me assure you, I have recovered.'

'I was trying to protect you, Antonia.'

'I don't need that sort of protection, Ra'id. I need to face life, however ugly it is.' And it was ugly sometimes, Antonia thought, as an image of her mother as a very young girl, writing down her deepest thoughts and fears because she had no one to confide in, appeared to be.

'I have your best interests at heart.'

'And thought you could woo me with expensive trinkets and the promise of more money than I could spend? Do you really think you can buy me, Ra'id?'

'I'm doing everything I can think of to reassure you.'

'To reassure me that it will be cosy in my gilded cage?' Antonia's voice broke as she shook her head in despair. 'You really don't know me.' Would Ra'id never be Saif again? Would he never hear her again?

'I'm prepared to give you everything I thought you wanted,' he said.

In fairness, that was exactly the type of girl she'd been, Antonia reflected. How long had her journey been? And how short was Ra'id's? Very short, she concluded. Nothing about the all-powerful ruler of Sinnebar had changed. What was he thinking now? She could usually read him, but today that famous connection of theirs had interference on the line. Something big was brewing. Ra'id would never have left her side for a minute if it had not been to make some special plan.

'I want nothing but the best for you.'

'And the best is to be your prisoner, because I'm carrying the heir to the throne?' Ra'id's expression stopped her. She had come here with him willingly, and in doing had crossed into dangerous, uncharted territory—to take on a man who was accustomed to his every word being law. Ra'id frightened her, but her fierce maternal instinct turned out to be stronger. Brandishing her mother's note at him, she demanded, 'Have we learned nothing from this, Ra'id? Am I to be kept in a palace as my mother was—another bird in a gilded cage, awaiting the sheikh's pleasure, while you carry on as normal?' Shaking her head decisively, she exclaimed, 'I won't do it!'

'Think, Antonia.'

'Oh, believe me, I've thought about this. Why would I agree to your plan when my only purpose in life would be to perfect the art of becoming invisible? I'd spend every day waiting for you, never knowing if you would turn up.'

'You're growing hysterical. You will have the charity to occupy your time, and very soon your child.'

'A child to *occupy* me?' Antonia protested in outrage. 'Looking after my baby will be a privilege. Yes, I'm expecting motherhood to be demanding, but never a chore—never something to *fill in my time*. A child is far too precious for that, Ra'id—something I don't expect you to understand.'

'I understand more than you know.'

Something about the way he spoke sent a flash of guilt through her, and then she realised he was thinking about Razi, the half-brother Ra'id had brought up when his mother had been driven away and his father had cared for no one but himself. 'I'm sorry. I should never have said that. I'm just—'

'Frightened of taking a step into the unknown?' Ra'id suggested. 'Your life doesn't have to be a repeat of the past, Antonia.' He glanced at the sheet of paper she was still holding clenched in her hand. 'The path you decide to take from here is up to you, and not some letter written years ago.'

'You would allow me to choose that path?'

'Why are you so certain I want to crush you?'

'I don't know, Ra'id. Maybe it has something to do with the fact that you led me to understand our child would live with you?'

'I would never agree to a child of mine living apart from me.'

'So you would never agree to live apart from your child, but I must?' Her voice shook as he touched on her Achilles heel.

'You will have full access, naturally.'

'And for that I must be grateful?'

'For that you must obey.'

So there it was, Antonia thought, turning pale. After all

the niceties and tactics were out of the way. Ra'id was a desert king, a warrior; a man she was only coming to know. 'This is your country where I must live by your rules and forget that I was ever free?' When he didn't answer, she added passionately, 'I'm not my mother, Ra'id. I'm not Helena. I'm not looking to escape, or excuse, and I'm certainly not looking for a man to keep me. I'm going to stay here and work to make the best use I can of my inheritance.'

'But that's what I want too. I have a hunting lodge in mind where you can stay until the work here is completed.'

'A hunting lodge, hidden away? Is that so different?' She gestured around and then let her arms drop to her side. She wanted to stay and work as a team, as they had on the island, not because she wanted to profit from it in any way but because she loved him and wanted to be with him.

'I'll leave you to think about it.'

She might have matured and learned from her mother's mistakes, but Ra'id would never change, Antonia realised as he ducked his head to leave the pavilion. This was the man she had fallen in love with: a king; an autocratic ruler; a man who was master of all he surveyed.

But not her master, Antonia determined when Ra'id had been gone for some time and she'd had time to cool down. Mounting up, she pointed her kindly gelding in the direction of the fort. She would plough her own furrow, however long that took.

CHAPTER SIXTEEN

ANTONIA had looked stricken when he had left her in the pavilion, while he felt not a moment's guilt. He had tried the softly-softly approach, and much as he had expected it had got him nowhere. It was time to return to his default setting of intractable command. What he had planned for Antonia's future was not only for the best for all of them, it was the only way they could move forward. She could take it or fight back, but conflict between them would only mean an unnecessary delay in her settling-in process.

She had accused him of being incapable of feeling, and maybe once he would have agreed with her. But his life had changed on the day a young virago had accosted him with a knife. Since then he felt everything acutely. Taking care of Antonia was his primary concern, but the luxury of showing his feelings was the one privilege he did not enjoy.

So maybe he had to lighten up? Allow Antonia to take more risks?

The one thing he was determined on was that Antonia would never take another risk and would not be put in danger. She might be a formidable force in the making, but if she was going to fulfil her potential she had to stay on track—and that was a track only Antonia could find. She thought he meant to keep her captive, when he knew that only the hand of life could contain her. Staying in Sinnebar or going back to Rome was Antonia's choice, though he dearly wanted her to stay. But a royal child? On that there could be no compromise. His child would be brought up by him, under his roof and under his protection.

He was leaning against the trunk of a palm-tree, staring out at the desert, when he saw her mounting up. He couldn't say it surprised him. Nothing about Antonia surprised him. For the sake of the horse he was glad she was lightweight. The gelding was moving well at the moment, but he had bathed its foreleg earlier, having noticed the first signs of trouble. He doubted she would get far, but he'd ride Tonnerre bareback and keep an eye on her.

So much for her brave adventure. Her horse went lame and she ended up leading it back to the pavilion. She could see Ra'id's stallion tethered nearby, but not Ra'id himself. Maybe he had summoned some super-silent high-tech helicopter to whisk him back to the capital. So much for his protective instincts; she'd be better off alone.

She trudged back to the pavilion, having fed and watered her horse, knowing her options were shrinking. What kind of future awaited her if she didn't sort this out? Would she be a prisoner like her mother? It had already begun—the waiting. Ra'id had said he'd be nearby, but he hadn't even tried to stop her leaving, and now he'd gone.

Entering the silent pavilion, she tugged off her boots. Exhausted by everything that had happened that day, she just about managed to strip off her clothes before tumbling into a disillusioned ball on top of the silken cushions, where she quickly fell asleep.

She was dreaming of riding in front of a mysterious, dark stranger on a wild, black stallion across mile upon mile of desert when the sound of rustling skirts shocked her awake. Blinking against the light, she sat up, and it took her a moment to realise three women were bowing to her. 'Please,' she begged them groggily as she hastily dragged a sheet over her naked body. She whisked her hand around to mime that no one had to bow to her.

As the kohl-lined eyes smiled back at her, Antonia recognised the three Bedouin women she'd met a couple of days before. 'I know you!' she said, putting two and two together and realising that Ra'id must have left her to ask them to come and keep her company. 'My riding clothes.' She pointed to them, and the women nodded with enthusiasm, their ice-blue robes with the intricate silver cross-stitch decoration twinkling in the strengthening light as Antonia thanked them for lending her such sensible clothes.

Now she was a little embarrassed, and had to carefully manoeuvre herself off the bed. Wrapping the cover tightly around her, she did her best to make them welcome. 'Would you like a drink?' she offered, lifting the jug of juice that had miraculously appeared on a nearby pierced-brass table.

The women must have brought it while she was asleep, Antonia realised, along with the dishes of sweetmeats and fruit. 'You're very generous,' she said, bowing to them as best she could in her sheet ensemble.

The women giggled, as if she was the funniest thing they had ever seen and, shaking their heads, indicated that first she must follow them.

The bathing pool had been warmed by the fast-strengthening sun, and Antonia exclaimed with surprise and pleasure to see the women had scattered rose petals on the surface of the water. This was real luxury, she thought, quite excited at having her hair washed and then her scalp massaged with the most sweet-smelling products. The world should know about these, Antonia decided when the women explained to her with mimed actions that they had picked and prepared the herbs and flowers for the lotions themselves. Maybe that was something else she could do when she wasn't busy with the baby, the restoration work and the charity.

When they had patted her dry with soft towels, warm hands massaged her with more fragrant unguents. This should be part of her daily routine—not that she'd have time, Antonia thought with a rueful smile. And what was coming next? she wondered when the women slipped a plain, loose robe over her head.

Taking her by the hands, they ushered her excitedly into the pavilion, where they sat her down and dried and polished her hair before plaiting it loosely and decorating it with exotic flowers. More scent was applied, until Antonia decided she smelled like a garden, and then they put make-up on her and painted intricate designs on her hands and feet with henna.

This really was special attention, she thought, starting to wonder about it—but then they produced another robe for her approval, and she gasped. The women were pleased to see her delight at this first sight of a masterpiece of design in sky-blue silk chiffon. The delicate fabric floated as they showed it to her, and was decorated with tiny seed-pearls and sparkling silver coins that would jingle as she moved. Before she put it on, the women fastened anklets of jewelled bells above her feet, and more around her wrists, and then they slipped the whisper of highly decorated silk-chiffon over her head. She was just revelling in those silken folds when, with some ceremony, they prepared to veil her.

She felt a real frisson of excitement now, realising this must be the culmination of the ceremony. They had even brought a full-length mirror into the pavilion, and placed it in front of her so she could see the finished effect.

She looked amazing—amazingly different, Antonia realised, seeing sultry eyes she hardly recognised flashing back at her. But the question uppermost in her mind was why? Why now? Why were the women doing this for her? What was this all about? And how could she ask her newfound friends what was going on, when no one spoke the same language? She couldn't be so rude as to stop the women when they were having such fun attending to her—and, truthfully, so was she—but she couldn't deny a nagging sense of doubt that suggested she was being prepared to take on the role of His Imperial Majesty's concubine.

She would bring everything to a halt if that were the case, Antonia determined, but for now... The women carried a twinkling veil reverently over outstretched arms. To try it on, just once, was irresistible. The veil sparkled bewitchingly, exceeding any fantasy image she could ever have come up with—and were those tiny jewels sewn onto the floating panels? Blue-white diamonds? The veil was clearly precious and significant to the women, judging by the way they handled it.

And they weren't finished with her yet, Antonia realised when they had draped it over her head and shoulders. Now they were going to secure it with the most fabulous rope of turquoise-and-coral beads. The turquoise toned beautifully with the robe, while the coral could have been chosen to point up the warm-blush tint in her cheeks.

What on earth had she done to deserve this?

That was her first thought, and it was swiftly followed by *who is this?* as an older woman entered the tent.

The older woman shocked Antonia into silence by explaining that Signorina Antonia Ruggerio had been adopted as a daughter of her tribe. 'And my name is Mariam,' she said. 'I will be your advocate, should you require me in the discussions to come.'

What discussions? Antonia wondered. And she could speak for herself, though she nodded and smiled politely. It must be something to do with the charity, she reasoned. This was a culture she knew little about, and if she wanted to forge ahead with her work it would be wise to have an interpreter— at least until she was fluent in the language herself. But a daughter of the tribe? That was a good thing, wasn't it?

Mariam pretty much confirmed these thoughts, explaining that once the most powerful tribe in Sinnebar had accepted Antonia as a daughter she would have no trouble persuading the rest of the country to support her.

Well, anything that would help to spread the reach of the charity was a good thing, Antonia supposed. Learning that Ra'id was the head of this most powerful tribe came as no surprise—but if he was also the head of the ruling council, who was going to refuse him? 'How does that work?' Antonia murmured, thinking out loud.

With a faint smile and a low bow, the woman called Mariam walked gracefully out of the pavilion.

Ruling council, my foot! Antonia thought, starting to pace. Once again, everything had been decided by Ra'id. She could see the point of the fabulous costume now. This wasn't a treat, it was a set-up, a shrewd move by Ra'id to involve her in some ceremony far away from the prying eyes of the world in an exotic setting he believed would seduce her. The ceremony probably wasn't even legal. She would be no more secure than her mother—no more visible, certainly. So much for her fantasy of the silken veil! She would be a prisoner in a silken veil, Ra'id's love-slave, until he tired of her.

She whirled around when he strode into the tent. 'Ra'id!' Mariam had entered behind him, and she was followed by the girls who had helped to prepare Antonia for their sheikh.

Ra'id stood in the centre of the pavilion, an ominous force dressed all in black, still with the *howlis* wrapped round his face. 'From now on,' he informed her, 'this is how it will be. These women will wait on you and I will not see you alone again until we are married.'

'Married?' The word choked off any air supply she might have had in her lungs.

'That is what you wanted, isn't it?' And before she could protest—*Yes! No! Not like this!*—he went on, 'Now you are an accepted daughter of the tribe, I must observe the formalities laid down.'

'Centuries ago?' Antonia challenged him, almost beside herself with shock.

'Oh no,' Ra'id replied evenly. 'Somewhat longer than that, I should think.'

'You are joking?' Then, realising the women standing behind Ra'id were still waiting for her instruction, Antonia remembered her manners and invited them to sit down.

Once everyone was seated, she went up to Ra'id; staring into his eyes, which was all she could see of his fierce face behind the headdress, she hissed, 'Did you think to ask me first? Did I miss something before you disappeared yesterday?'

The expression in Ra'id's eyes remained as shrewd and as dangerous as ever. 'I thought you liked surprises,' he said mildly.

'Some surprises,' Antonia agreed. But surprises came in many forms. The chance to dress up in pretty clothes was nice, but when it came to matters of the heart—things that really mattered—like a marriage between two people…

She'd done with surprises, Antonia realised. It would be helpful if an alarm rang on the day you grew up, she reflected—helpful to everyone, especially Ra'id. She could no longer be seduced by a visit behind the silken veil, or by fabulous jewels and clothes that looked as if they had been sequestered from the set of a Hollywood movie. Or by some hasty marriage ceremony that probably had no legal standing outside this tent. Before she'd come to Sinnebar? Yes; she had been impressionable then, before she had met and fallen in love with a man called Saif. But now there was just one man and one woman, or there should have been. And you could forget the trimmings; she didn't need them. She would never settle for anything less than a real marriage based on love. She certainly didn't intend to be bulldozed into the most important decision of her life just because this was expedient for Ra'id.

'What do you think you're doing?' he demanded as she started tugging off the rope of jewels holding her veil in place.

Ra'id had underestimated her for the last time, Antonia determined. 'If you don't know…' she said, and then, conscious that they weren't alone, she added more discreetly, 'Do you mind if we walk outside? Only I'm feeling a little faint in here.'

'Of course.'

Ra'id was immediately concerned about her.

About her *pregnancy*, and the welfare of his child, Antonia amended as the ruler of Sinnebar escorted her out of the tent.

He was at her side in a moment. Pregnancy must have weakened her, he realized. There was some shade inside the pavilion, but no air-conditioning, plus he and the other women were used to the heat.

Having removed her veil and carefully placed the rope of precious jewels on top of it, she took a moment to reassure the women and thank them by miming with expressive hands. They looked at him for reassurance too, and with a brief dip of his chin as he strode past them he confirmed Antonia's wishes. This was not the child-woman he had first encountered on his yacht, but a woman of purpose who made her own decisions.

She made for a group of palm trees where he had sheltered the previous evening and there she stopped. 'What's wrong?' he said, joining her in the shade.

'This—all this,' she said with a sweep of her hands over the jewelled gown. 'More toys for me to play with, Ra'id? I grew up with this—I thought you knew that. I have fourteen wardrobes crammed full of clothes back in Rome. My brother gives me everything that money can buy; at one time I thought that beautiful clothes and wonderful jewellery, eating at the best places in Rome, was all it took to make me happy. I took it for granted, because that was my life. But it's not enough, Ra'id. I've seen more now, and I want more.'

'More?' He hated the disillusionment spilling from Antonia's lips, though he wondered if he had ever seen her looking lovelier than she did now with the morning breeze tossing her hair about and a vision of the future in her eyes.

'I don't mean more stuff,' she said, perhaps sounding younger than she had intended. 'I mean more time to be us—to be real—to do real things.'

'If you mean time to work for the good of the charity?' he said.

'Yes!' she exclaimed. 'If you'll let me work for Sinnebar, I'll put my whole heart into it. I don't need this pomp and ceremony, Ra'id. And, as for becoming a daughter of the tribe, it's very kind of you—but it's too late for me to become anyone's daughter. I'm not a child any longer, Ra'id. Can't you see that?'

His proposal for the tribe to adopt her had been his way of smoothing Antonia's path so that they could be married. He had come to this conclusion without consulting her, he realised now. He hadn't even told her how empty his life would be without her. In fact, life without Antonia was unthinkable. But had he told her that? Slowly unwinding his *howlis*, he stood staring out at the desert over which he ruled. He had made much of that desert into a garden for his people to enjoy and to nurture and harvest crops on. Was there as much hope for him?

Then she placed her hand on his arm and stared up at him, pleading. 'Don't drive me away.'

'That's the very last thing I'm trying to do.'

'Then you must know I would never settle for anything less than a marriage based on love?'

Ra'id held her gaze. He looked more magnificent than she had ever seen him. There wasn't a single item of his clothing, or even his expression, his hair or his eyes, that wasn't unrelieved black, but she loved him without fear or favour. What did his outer coating matter? When she had seen him in regal robes of royal blue trimmed with golden thread and yellow sapphire, had she loved him more? Saif, in his worn, frayed shorts and faded top was the man she had fallen in love with, and they were one and the same. Except, Ra'id al Maktabi was a man turned hard by duty. But Ra'id's fearful title didn't frighten her. She wouldn't allow anything to stand in the way of the people they could be. 'You were wrong about me liking surprises,' she told him softly. Still with her hand resting on Ra'id's arm, she explained, 'There are some surprises I do not like at all.'

Her heart faltered when he looked down at her and then she saw Saif in his eyes. 'I think I get that,' he said.

'Can we talk?' she whispered, hardly daring to believe what was happening.

'We can talk,' Ra'id confirmed, and, finding her hand with his, he linked their fingers together and, turning, they slowly walked together back to the tent.

He dismissed the servants so he and Antonia could be together.

'It will cost you nothing,' she told him earnestly, fixing her gaze on his. 'No jewels, no land grants, nothing except you and me together, forging a future.'

He heard the question in her voice, and it was a question he couldn't wait to answer. Drawing her to him, he kissed her gently on the brow. 'Your wish is my command,' he murmured.

He had dreams too, and his dream had grown to encompass the two of them standing together—but not too close for, in the words of the poet, even the pillars of the temple stood apart.

CHAPTER SEVENTEEN

THE VALUE of a hug could not be overestimated, Antonia realised as Ra'id held her close. Sometimes she needed a hug more than anything, and it turned out that Ra'id was really good at that too. They were talking now and he was listening, really listening; she was back with the man she loved, the man she had known as Saif. She had changed into a casual robe and was reclining on the cushions with Ra'id, staring out across the ocean of sand through the silken curtain that covered the entrance to his pavilion. 'I could never live as my mother lived.'

'You won't have to. And, before you accuse me of fiendish plots and insurmountable character-flaws, let me reassure you that I do understand love. I also understand that love takes many forms and that sometimes fate doesn't allow enough time for love to be proven.'

'You're not defending your father, I hope?'

'He gave your mother land. People show their love in different ways, Antonia, and though I think my father loved himself best of all I also think he finally discovered a conscience.'

'But he abandoned his son, Razi, for reasons of self-interest.'

'I can't argue with you on that point, but neither can I continue to believe that your mother didn't care for you.'

'What?' Antonia turned to him in surprise.

'She must have done.'

'Or wanted to cause the maximum upheaval in Sinnebar as some sort of revenge.'

'Isn't it time to give her the benefit of the doubt?'

'I never thought I'd hear you defending her.' This was the pivotal moment, Antonia felt, when Ra'id would make sense of her past as she was beginning to understand his.

'Helena must have known her life in Sinnebar would end some day.'

'And in such a terrible way—locked up, incarcerated, forgotten. No wonder she bolted into the arms of my father.'

Ra'id nodded 'Your mother escaped, as she saw it. And went on to make your father very happy, I believe. And when your mother wrote her will she wanted to be sure her children had something significant to remember her by.'

'Her land in Sinnebar? But in leaving it to her children she must have known how much trouble that would cause.'

'In Sinnebar when a parent dies their property is divided equally between their surviving children, so Helena had no choice in the matter. And, maybe, the country meant more to Helena than we know. She had that friendship with her maidservant, remember? Maybe Helena was just starting to grow up when my father decided he was tired of her.'

'I can't believe you're taking her side,' Antonia said, feeling as if a great weight had been lifted from her shoulders.

'Why should you find it so hard to believe? You're Helena's daughter. I have to believe there was some good in her—unexplored possibilities.'

They remained quiet for a while, and then she said softly, 'Thank you, Ra'id. I understand now why you wanted to be with me when I read that page from my mother's diary.' But she was thanking Ra'id for more than that, Antonia realised; she was thanking him for his ability to see through the muddle of the past to a place from where they could both move forward.

'Don't forget this when you put that page away safely, will you?'

Antonia gasped when she saw the necklace Ra'id was holding out to her. 'Where did you find that?'

'It dropped into my hand,' he said, tongue in cheek.

She blushed. 'I hope you don't think…'

'That you stole it?' With a wry smile, he shook his head and then handed her the slender chain with the diamond-studded heart dangling from it. 'This has always belonged to you, along with the rest of your mother's possessions. I can only apologise that, like anything else that was left behind, it wasn't found earlier and sent to you in Rome.'

'I'm rather glad it wasn't,' Antonia admitted, knowing this was a much better way to receive it. 'And you've mended it!' she exclaimed.

Reaching behind her neck as Ra'id fastened the clasp for her, she rested her hand on his. 'Do you think your father gave this to my mother?'

'Who knows? And does it matter?' he said. 'All that matters is that you have it now. I believe your mother would have wanted that.'

'You really are turning into a romantic.'

'Let's not get carried away,' Ra'id cautioned. 'A few romantic minutes a day are the most I can manage.'

'So, not long enough—' She had been about to say 'for a wedding', and only just managed to stop herself in time.

But Ra'id would not be distracted. 'Not long enough for what?' he said. 'What were you about to say to me, Antonia?'

'Nothing,' she said, but her blazing cheeks gave her away. 'Do I expect too much?'

Antonia's face was as serious as he had ever seen it; this was the closest they had ever been, and she needed him to be absolutely honest with her. 'You've certainly tested me to the limits of my endurance.'

'I don't know what you mean.'

'Yes, you do,' he said, his lips tugging in a smile. 'Why don't you test me again?' he suggested. And this time she knew exactly what he meant.

It was much later when he caused her to cry out again, and this time with surprise. 'Sorry,' he mocked gently, removing the velvet box from her hand before she had a chance to open it. 'I forgot you don't like surprises.'

'Just a minute,' she admonished him, sitting bolt-upright, naked and beautiful. 'Like you said about love, surprises come in many forms—and some of them aren't so bad.'

'Well, if you're sure?' he said, pressing his lips down in a pretence of doubt as he opened the catch on the velvet box to reveal the magnificent royal-blue sapphire surrounded by blue-white diamonds he had picked out in the hope that Antonia would wear it on her wedding finger.

'Are you suggesting a partnership?' she said, narrowing her eyes.

'I was rather thinking a marriage. Isn't that the same thing?'

'No, it isn't the same thing at all,' she assured him with all the defiance in her voice that he loved.

'A marriage and a partnership, then?' he amended.

'If I can have both…' She appeared to think about it.

'If I can have you standing beside me, you can have anything,' Ra'id said.

'In that case…'

'I love you,' he said simply as she threw herself into his arms. 'I love you and I want to marry you, Antonia. Unfortunately that means you will have to be a queen, and for that I apologise. I know you, above all people, understand what is involved in loving a country and its people as I do.'

'And I love its king,' she assured him. 'But, most of all, I love you…Saif, Ra'id, Sword of Vengeance—whoever you are.' And then she laughed and warned him, 'You'd better not use that sword on anyone else, or you're in serious trouble.'

'Grow up,' he said, tumbling her onto the cushions.

'In that respect? Never,' she promised him defiantly.

Then he kissed her with all the passion with which only Ra'id was capable, and in a way that convinced Antonia she'd found not her lover, or even her husband, but her soul mate; there could be no other. Ra'id had kissed the last of her fears away until she was triumphant and strong. There was only one thing missing, Antonia realised as Ra'id pulled away.

But then he did that too.

'Antonia Ruggiero,' he whispered, kneeling in front of her with his head bowed. 'Would you do me the honour of becoming my wife?'

'Yes…Oh, yes!' she exclaimed.

'Will you be my queen, the mother of my children, and will you work at my side for the good of Sinnebar?' Ra'id demanded, lifting his proud, formidably handsome face to stare her in the eyes. 'Because I love you—and will always love you.'

'I will,' she said fearlessly. 'I will.'

Moving to embrace her, Ra'id cupped her face in his hands. 'If you look with your heart, you will find as I did that the most important things in life aren't land or possessions, they're invisible.'

'As long as *I'm* not invisible.'

'You, Antonia?' Ra'id's expression changed from irony to sincerity. 'You could never be ignored—you'd make sure of that. But please be serious for a moment. I'm saying I love you, and I'll take a lifetime to prove it to you if I have to. And, as for the land, it will always be yours—'

'Or I could give it to the people of Sinnebar,' she interrupted him, which felt right to her.

A faint smile tugged at Ra'id's firm mouth. 'Now do you see why I love you?' he said, and, taking the fabulous sapphire ring out of its velvet nest, he placed it on Antonia's wedding finger.

EPILOGUE

SHE couldn't have everything her own way.

Which wasn't such a bad thing, Antonia conceded, staring at her wedding dress twinkling in the faint, pink light before dawn. Ra'id had insisted that their people required their queen to look like a queen, and that Antonia could have her wedding dress adapted at some later stage and wear it again if she felt bad about the extravagance.

It was a dream of a dress, Antonia reflected, holding back the folds of the lavish bridal-pavilion where she had spent the night. She had tumbled out of bed in time to see Ra'id leave the encampment. He had galloped away on his fierce black stallion, with his younger brother Razi at his side, their very masculine silhouettes framed against a brightening sky as they rode across the brow of the dune. They were two unimaginably powerful men like heroes of old, leaning low over the necks of their straining horses as they raced away, no doubt to enjoy an early-morning swim in some lush, green oasis.

The wedding gown the tribeswomen had created for their queen was an exquisite column of a dress in heavy ivory silk, embroidered for this occasion in gold thread by

specialist craftswomen who lived deep in the interior of
Sinnebar. It managed to be both demure and sexy, with
long sleeves to preserve Antonia's modesty, but body-
skimming to hint at what lay beneath. She hoped Ra'id
would take the hint, as they hadn't made love since their
last night in the desert. Far from dulling her sexual urges,
pregnancy had only made her hungrier for him, a fact she
was sure he knew, but which he cruelly refused to take
action on. The thought that this would be their wedding
night made desire cry deep inside her, and it was a voice
she was determined he would hear.

The sexual tension between them had become unbearable, Antonia realised as she walked deeper into the luxurious womb-like interior of her tent. The bridal pavilion
was decorated in many shades of crimson, fuchsia and
rose-pink silk, and was a delicately scented sanctuary
where she was supposed to be resting before the rigours of
their week-long marriage ceremony. But wanting Ra'id
made rest impossible. It felt as if they were starting over
from the moment they had met. Her body yearned for him
so shamelessly, only now it was worse, because now she
knew what she was missing.

The wedding ceremony was to be at dawn and already
a tented city had grown up on the ivory-sugar sand. Lights
glinted as far as the eye could see, as Ra'id's subjects had
gathered from every corner of the kingdom to see him wed
the girl who had laboured night and day at their side to
prepare the renovated fort for the first of the children it
would house. Antonia had wanted to name the centre after
her mother, but the people had ruled that they would name
it after her. Ra'id had compromised when he'd opened the

Queen Antonia Children's Centre, adding a small plaque signed by Antonia in memory of Helena Ruggiero that said quite simply: *She looked into the future and believed.*

That plaque was the best gift Ra'id could ever have given her, Antonia reflected, gazing at the casket of fabulous jewels he had given her the previous evening. She smiled, remembering him commanding her not to take them off during their wedding ceremony, as she had removed her jewels once before. 'Our people must see you,' Ra'id had insisted, when she protested at the size and quantity of the sparking diamonds.

'They'll hardly miss me wearing these,' she had replied, touching the glittering stones he had fastened around her neck. 'They must be worth a king's ransom.'

'No—a sheikh's,' he had told her dryly. 'You may consider me your hostage for life.'

She would, Antonia thought, hugging herself in anticipation.

She turned at the sound of footsteps. The women had come for her, she noticed, her excitement mounting as they slipped silently into the pavilion. She still couldn't believe they had come to dress their queen.

They bathed her, prepared her, scented her and polished her, until her skin glowed and her body yearned for the touch of Ra'id—her lover, her soul mate, her king. They laced the diamonds in her hair and arranged her filmy, ivory-coloured veil beneath them—the veil that Ra'id would remove in their wedding tent prior to…

The sound of the *nafir*, the horn with a single true note, was a fortunate disruption to Antonia's progressively sensual thoughts. There were people to greet, and a ceremony

to undergo with grace and dignity, before the longed-for
moment when she could be alone with Ra'id.

And when that moment came she trembled like a virgin.
Or, at least, that was how she felt as Ra'id removed her veil
with a teasing lack of speed. She felt like a virgin waiting
to be kissed by her lover for the very first time. But when
Ra'id kissed her brow, and then the swell of her belly
where their baby lay safe and loved, she knew this was
going to be better and far deeper than anything she had experienced before.

'Our child,' he murmured, sharing her sense of wonder.

'Our family,' she answered, quivering with enough expectation to found a dynasty as Ra'id's lips brushed her
mouth. That kiss was all the more arousing for his lack of
haste or pressure, she realised, shivering with frustration
beneath Ra'id's tantalisingly light touch.

'We have all the time in the world,' he murmured,
teasing her as he always did.

'Don't make me wait that long,' Antonia protested,
while Ra'id laughed. And, falling back on the bed, he drew
her on top of him. 'Tiger woman.'

'Meets rampant lion?' she suggested, tracing the lines
of the tattoo on Ra'id's chest.

'An interesting coupling,' he agreed.

'Let's find out, shall we?' Antonia suggested, slipping
out of her fabulous robe.

millsandboon.co.uk Community

Join Us!

The Community is the perfect place to meet and chat to kindred spirits who love books and reading as much as you do, but it's also the place to:

- Get the inside scoop from authors about their latest books
- Learn how to write a romance book with advice from our editors
- Help us to continue publishing the best in women's fiction
- Share your thoughts on the books we publish
- Befriend other users

Forums: Interact with each other as well as authors, editors and a whole host of other users worldwide.

Blogs: Every registered community member has their own blog to tell the world what they're up to and what's on their mind.

Book Challenge: We're aiming to read 5,000 books and have joined forces with The Reading Agency in our inaugural Book Challenge.

Profile Page: Showcase yourself and keep a record of your recent community activity.

Social Networking: We've added buttons at the end of every post to share via digg, Facebook, Google, Yahoo, technorati and de.licio.us.

www.millsandboon.co.uk

2 FREE BOOKS
AND A SURPRISE GIFT

We would like to take this opportunity to thank you for reading this Mills & Boon® book by offering you the chance to take TWO more specially selected books from the Modern™ series absolutely FREE! We're also making this offer to introduce you to the benefits of the Mills & Boon® Book Club™—

- **FREE home delivery**
- **FREE gifts and competitions**
- **FREE monthly Newsletter**
- **Exclusive Mills & Boon Book Club offers**
- **Books available before they're in the shops**

Accepting these FREE books and gift places you under no obligation to buy, you may cancel at any time, even after receiving your free books. Simply complete your details below and return the entire page to the address below. You don't even need a stamp!

YES Please send me 2 free Modern books and a surprise gift. I understand that unless you hear from me, I will receive 4 superb new books every month for just £3.19 each, postage and packing free. I am under no obligation to purchase any books and may cancel my subscription at any time. The free books and gift will be mine to keep in any case.

Ms/Mrs/Miss/Mr _____ Initials _____

Surname _____

Address _____

_____ Postcode _____

E-mail _____

Send this whole page to: Mills & Boon Book Club, Free Book Offer, FREEPOST NAT 10298, Richmond, TW9 1BR

Offer valid in UK only and is not available to current Mills & Boon Book Club subscribers to this series. Overseas and Eire please write for details.. We reserve the right to refuse an application and applicants must be aged 18 years or over. Only one application per household. Terms and prices subject to change without notice. Offer expires 30th June 2010. As a result of this application, you may receive offers from Harlequin Mills & Boon and other carefully selected companies. If you would prefer not to share in this opportunity please write to The Data Manager, PO Box 676, Richmond, TW9 1WU.